Annie

....

Barbara Brums

Contents

1

I bit my cheek as my leg bounced uncontrollably against the car seat. I had been staring outside the window without blinking the entire ride. Every inch of my body felt like it was vibrating and not even my tightly wrung hands could keep it in check. I untucked and re-tucked my hair for the umpteenth time as we pulled into the parking lot and against the curb.

"Annie," Serena's voice called, but even as I turned my head to look at her, my eyes remained glazed over and unfocused. "I know you're nervous and...", she hesitated, "scared."

A breath left my lips as I turned my head back to look at the daunting building before me. In this moment, scared felt like a severe understatement.

Serena continued, "I know you're going to do well here. You are such a strong girl, so much stronger than I think even you know."

"I can't do it." The words left me instinctively. It wasn't just that I felt it, it's that I knew it deep down in my bones, in my soul, in every inch of my being. I wasn't ready yet. It was too soon. I haven't finished grieving yet.

"Yes. You can." Serena's words laced in finality. "I know this is a push for you but it's one I know you need. I wouldn't do it if I wasn't certain it was something you could handle."

I chanced a glance back at Serena's face. Dark black hair framed her face in a neat, slightly wavy bob. Her dark brown eyes were warm like honey and the softness in which she looked at me spoke more to me than her words. Her cherry red lips quirked into a gentle smile, a gentle plead.

We may not be related by blood but she was the closest thing to family I have ever had. Not even 6 months since taking me in, letting me move into her home and become her legal responsibility, and she was the woman who cared about me more deeply than anyone ever before. I was forever indebted to Serena, whether she thought about it that way or not.

"I don't think this will make me get better." I whispered. An admission from the inner workings of my mind - a place I rarely invited Serena into.

"How do you know if you are so unwilling to try?" Serena reached out and smoothed the back of my hair, her touch as gentle as her voice.

I gulped, shakily grabbing the strap of the pink backpack that laid at my feet.

I wasn't going to do this for me. Doing it for myself would not be enough to convince me to walk in there - let alone to even get out of this car. Going in there for Serena, though? She deserved that much and so much more. She deserved me to give this a genuine effort after all the trouble I've already put her through.

On the count of three, before I completely lost my nerve, I opened the car door and stepped out. Swinging my bag over my shoulder, I closed the car door behind me before I could change my mind. Serena seemed to be thinking along the same lines because before I could take another second to think about what I'd just done, she was already pulling away from the curve and driving off with a gentle wave 'goodbye.'

I blinked and then blinked again.

My mind was working overtime trying to understand what I had just done. My mouth was slightly agape, dumbfounded. The pace of my heartbeat was quickening and suddenly I was too aware of my entire being.

I dared a glance to both my left and right.

Not many people were here yet. I was grateful then that Serena had decided to drop me off extra early so that I could get my schedule squared away. Most teenagers didn't bother coming to school this early, certainly not if they didn't have to.

I dug my fingernails into both my palms, willing myself to start walking. My eyes darted all around me now. I felt increasingly exposed by the second. Consciously I knew that even as I walked, nobody was really looking my way. Unconsciously, that didn't stop the rising panic I felt in the form of bile hitting the back of my throat.

Forcing it down, I willed myself to enter my new high school.

The hallway almost felt worse than outside. Tiny walk ways crammed with lockers against the walls on each side, I started feeling slightly dizzy. This time I kept my head down as I walked through as fast as I could. Maybe not seeing anything but my shoes on the shiny, squeaky floor was the best way I was going to get through this.

My hands trembled by the time I reached the main office. I was almost drunk on relief once the door clicked shut behind me and I was nearly alone. The only other person being a short middle-aged woman typing away at her computer on the front desk.

I barely managed a step her way before her eyes snapped to me.

"Can I help you, dear?" The woman's cheerful voice reached me.

"Oh - I - um this is my first day and I need my -" I stuttered over myself, still a bit distressed from my walk here.

"Schedule." The lady finished my sentence for me. She smiled brightly and started typing away on her computer before speaking again, "Your name, hun?"

"Annie-"

"Thatcher," She cut me off once more. "Goodness me, let's see where I put this thing. Aha here it is." She beamed.

I could only stare at her with wide-eyes as she printed out my schedule. How she had so much energy this early in the morning was beyond me, even if it did work to make me feel slightly more at ease than I was in the hallway.

"Okay, here you go. Theres even a map on the back for you. Let me know if you have any more questions, dear. I am always here and happy to help." She sent me another blinding smile, only working to make me believe her words that much more, before turning her attention back to the computer before her.

I hesitated.

Our interaction had been far quicker than I had anticipated. I hadn't mentally prepared myself to go back out into that hallway so soon. Especially now that more students had certainly shown up in the time I'd been in here. I looked around the office in a slight panic, my cheeks surely turning the ugliest shade of red like they always did. My hands clutched the paper schedule so tight, I was almost positive that I ripped it some.

"Hun?" The woman's voice drew me back to her instantly. "Did you need something else?" She asked, looking far more concerned now than she had before. I must have looked just as bad as I was starting to feel, only managing to make me feel that much worse.

I tried to clear my dry throat, searching for my voice. "I don't know if I'll be able to find my classes." I spoke slightly above a whisper. It was a pathetic excuse considering the map that I currently held in my hands, the map that I hadn't even spared a look at, but it was the best my muddled mind could come up with. It wasn't as if I was lying either.

"It is quite confusing isn't it?" She said, laughing slightly to herself before continuing, "I keep telling Principle Hendrick that it needs to be redone - simplified - but he doesn't have it high on his list of priorities at the moment. Completely understandable, of course. It takes a lot to make this school run smoothly." She chuckled again and then sighed. "Anyways, what can we do about this?" She hummed, tapping her pen against the counter as she frowned in thought.

I hadn't noticed the door opened again until the woman's eyes focused on something behind me. I was about to turn around when I felt a large presence brush past me. A waft of cool air from the hallway passing with the stranger.

"Oh Knox!" The woman called enthusiastically. "The timing is simply perfect, really. Annie here is new and needs someone to help her find her way around." The woman beamed.

"I'm not on the welcoming committee." He answered back blandly. His voice was gritty as if it was the first time he had used it all morning.

At this the woman became more serious than I had ever seen her yet this morning, "I'm sure our dear Principle Hendrick would be a lot easier on your whole situation with Liam if you did this favor."

I stood, staring at the interaction with wide eyes and a pounding heart. My breathing only turned more shallow when the boy turned his head, briefly making eye contact with me. The gnawing feeling that burned deep in my chest was back with a vengeance. Whoever this boy was, he was stacked. Not that he had to be in order to strike fear in me. Just the look in his dark brown eyes was enough to have me wanting to shrink into my skin. Turning his back on me again, I could only further analyze his stature. He was almost a whole foot taller than me and was certainly double my width. His arms bulged and a tattoo that was barely visible from underneath the sleeve of his shirt snaked up his arm and out of sight.

He stepped forward, leaning against the counter now. Crossing his arms, his back flexed making me gulp.

"If I do this favor, all is forgiven?" He asked, his voice deepening in seriousness. It raised the hair on my arms, ticking me uncomfortably.

"I will see what I can do, Knox, but it would undoubtably help." She spoke pointedly.

The whole conversation had become unnerving. Whatever this boy, Knox, had done to get into this kind of trouble was enough to alarm me even further.

A tense moment of silence passed - or maybe it was only tense for me - before he answered.

"Yeah, alright." He grumbled, turning back around to face me.

I found myself struggling to breath yet again. I snapped the hair tie on my wrist, trying to wake myself up from whatever horrible nightmare I had landed myself in. It wasn't working, only making the skin of my wrist bright red.

"R-really, I don't need any help." I barely forced the words out of my mouth, coming out strained and hoarse.

Knox rolled his eyes, "You don't have to look like you've been sentenced to death." He approached me, pulling my schedule from between my fingers. My face reddened again upon seeing the crumpled mess it had become after being the main outlet of my stress.

"C'mon. Stay close. Bit of a free for all out there." Knox continued looking down at my schedule before stuffing it in his pocket and reaching out to open the office door.

He had not been exaggerating. Students flooded the hall and lined the walls in each direction. The shouts and loud talking was jarring in comparison to the quiet office I was being forced to leave.

I hadn't realized I was stuck in the door, unable to step out until I heard Knox directly behind me, making me jump.

"I know. Fuckin' animals, huh?" He meant it as a joke and maybe to anyone else it would have been, but the thought of being amongst said animals was entirely too terrifying.

I tried fighting back the tears that were now threatening to spill over and down my cheeks. I could feel Knox staring down at me, but I couldn't find myself to be too concerned over whatever he was thinking in that moment. He could judge me all he wanted, I had already come this far and that was accomplishment enough for me.

His fingers grazed the small of my back as if to start leading me forward. The simple action made me gasp and jump away from his touch, taken aback at jolt of electricity that raced through me.

Knox furrowed his brows and tried to mask his confusion quickly. "Just hold onto my backpack behind me. People usually stay out of my way." He recovered, his voice much softer than before.

I gazed up at him apprehensively but stiffly nodded my head nonetheless. Holding on to his backpack seemed a far better deal than having his hand on the small of my back. I took hold of one of the loose bottom parts of his backpack strap with both my hands.

Swiftly, Knox started walking with me on his heel. Just like he said, people cleared out from in front of him, making just enough room for us to make our way through unscathed. I probably shouldn't be as proud for making it through something as simple as a school hallway as I was but a win is a win.

Finally, he stopped outside was I could only assume would be my first class. He led me off to the side of the door, still away from anybody passing by.

"This is your first class," he nodded his head in the direction of the door, "don't leave until I come get you. It gets worse after first. Don't even leave your seat, Annie. I'll come get you." Knox emphasized.

I nodded my head, barely uttering a soft, "Okay", before heading inside.

2

The second that I entered my first class, history, I had already lost any last bits of confidence I thought I could retain.

The short-lived triumph of having made it through the hall and into this room was trumped by the intimidating men that already lingered in their picked seats. I eyed the row in the back, but luck was not on my side when my eyes met the group of boys who occupied them. I was then forced to opt for a seat closer to the front than I wanted.

I hoped being far away from the other boys in the back would make this choice worth it, but I was quickly found wrong.

The seat in front of me was taken within seconds. He was a dark-haired lanky boy who sat crookedly slouched. His shaggy hair gave away the, what I could only assume was unintentional, heavy tilt of his head.

He had no issues leaning as far back into his seat as he possibly could. The wisps of his long strands of hair danced across the edge of my desk as if taunting me.

I wiped my sweaty palms on my jean skirt and tried to follow his lead in leaning back in my own chair so as to create as much distance between the two of us as possible.

This didn't last long.

Another boy filled the seat behind me only a moment later. He moved so quickly, I could not catch more than a red blur and I was definitely not willing to turn my head even half a centimeter to subdue my curiosity in knowing what the rest of him looked like.

All that seemed to matter was the dull tapping of his foot against the leg of my chair, successfully managing to keep me on edge from the constant reminder of his presence throughout the entire class period. I couldn't even lean back in the chair any longer in fear that I would continue to feel his breath hitting the back of my neck. Instead, I sat stick-straight and rigid, afraid that any movement in either direction would bring me unbearably closer to either one of the two boys.

To say that I was distracted was an extreme understatement.

I was so caught up in my own internal struggle, I was still not even sure I caught my teacher's name correctly. Not to mention anything he was actually trying to teach us. Every word he spoke seemed to die just before it was supposed to reach my ears.

When the boy behind me finally stopped tapping his foot on my chair, I thought I would finally be able to gain some sense of awareness. Next thing I knew, everyone was filing out of the room even quicker than they had arrived.

I gripped the edge of the desk closest to me while everyone walked by. I kept my eyes concentrated on the grain, following the pattern of the wood as a way to distract myself. I wasn't sure how long I did it for but I suppose the whole exercise had worked a bit too well.

I nearly jumped out of my seat when two hands came down on the corners of the desk, a boy leaning down over me. My lips parted in an almost gasp and my eyes shot up to meet that of Knox's.

We kept eye contact for several endless moments, me just gaping up at him, until he finally spoke, "Are you going to stare at me all day or are we gonna go?"

"Go where?" I asked instinctively. As soon as the question left my lips, I blanched. It slipped off my tongue before I could stop it. I must have been so disoriented, or at least so mentally exhausted, that I forgot the entire reason I was enduring this torture to begin with.

"Your next class, no?" Knox asked, his tone and eyes laced with amusement.

I nodded but made no effort to move. I was still very much reeling from the past hour.

"C'mon, Annie."

Knox released his hold on my desk before leaning down and picking up my backpack that had been sitting next to the desk chair.

Numbly, as if I was a newborn deer, I wobbled on my legs as I stood back up again. Fitting my backpack back on, Knox's fingers brushed against the skin of my neck. I gasped at the sensation, having felt a trail of tingles where his finger had touched - or maybe I had just imagined it. Knox briefly raised an eyebrow at my gasp before heading to the door of the classroom.

He waited in the doorway until I caught up so I could take hold of the strap of his bag. It felt mildly demeaning, holding onto his backpack strap. It felt a bit like a leash, like I was being taken on a walk like a dog. Not that I necessarily thought he meant it this way but I felt embarrassed either way.

Knox glanced at me one more time as if checking that I was ready before he took a step out into the hallway.

I had forgotten Knox's words from earlier - forgotten that it would be worse than last time. I had not dwelled on this fact long enough to truly prepare myself for it. Body after body of students just wedged against each other, each trying to shove their way through the endless stream of people.

"No." I whispered, gripping the strap tighter as if Knox was now the dog on the leash and I was trying to force him to stop walking.

If Knox felt a tug, he didn't act like it. He was about to step out with me when I tugged harder, trying my best not to be pulled after him. I probably should have just let go instead. I should have just let Knox go by himself for as long as it would take him to notice I wasn't behind him. I definitely should not have gripped the strap tighter like I did.

There was no time to think about letting go by the time I had already committed to holding on tighter. I was already being pulled in after him. Right into the sea of bodies, boys and girls and everything in between pressed up against each other in every which direction.

I was pulled right into his back, hitting my face against the hard textbooks he was carrying inside his bag. I whimpered. An elbow quickly jabbed my back from someone trying to pass by. Then another one seconds later. Immediately being followed by a hard shove to my side.

I felt like I was choking. Tears were burring my vision and cascading down my face. My face, my back, and my side were stinging. I couldn't breathe. I needed to throw up. Something hit the back of my head forcing a sort of strangled cry out of my mouth.

I didn't know where I was anymore, didn't realize when we weren't in the crowd any longer. I could barely make out Knox's face when he looked down at me.

"Holy fuck. Annie, what's wrong?" His voice sounded so very distant.

I had no control of my senses anymore. I couldn't focus on anything except the incessant pounding of my head. Standing suddenly felt too difficult.

My knees buckled right out from under me. The only thing stopping me from slamming into the cold, hard tiles was Knox's quick reflexes in catching me. My vision then went completely black.

I opened my eyes in what felt like just a blink but I had far more trouble adjusting to the light. I had been laying down on something hard. All my limbs felt stiff as if they too had fallen asleep. There was a dull ringing in my ears. Slowly blinking, I started to sit up but felt another wave of dizziness.

"Woah, hun. Just stay laying down for now. Keep that ice pack steady on your forehead." A soft voice spoke, coming up next to me.

"Wh-what happened?" I croaked, my mouth and throat gone completely dry.

"Seems like you had a bit of a panic attack and passed out. You're alright, though. No apparent injuries seeing as you didn't hit anything on your way down." The woman spoke again.

My vision was still blurry and it felt like no amount of blinking was helping. My head was still pounding and my skin, it burned. As the memories of what happened came flooding in, the feeling of people hitting me - touching me - returned too.

"Home." I gasped, unable to choke out a full sentence. I was aching to be back in my room - back in my bed. I felt like I was choking again.

"Yes, let me go call your mom and I'll be right back, okay?" The nurse said as she handed me a glass of water, which I gulped down immediately, before she left the room.

The door hadn't even clicked closed before I heard another person walking in. My eyes found his immediately. I didn't need to have clear vision to know who it was.

"Annie..." Knox spoke, his voice trailing off.

"Thank you for catching me." I choked out in a scratchy whisper after a few moments of tense silence.

"Don't thank me, Annie." He all but ordered.

I gulped, understanding the look he was giving me all too well. He felt guilty. He came in here to apologize. I could see it, not written on his face, but in his eyes. I didn't want it, though. It wasn't his fault that I was so scared of being touched, I couldn't control myself. The last thing I wanted was his apology so I was glad when he didn't say it, at least not out loud.

Instead, Knox twirled a single strand of my hair around his index finger before dropping it and leaving the room entirely without another word.

3

- -

S erena had come to pick me up a short while later. She didn't ask me any questions when she picked me up nor once we got in the car. The entire ride was silent except for my occasional sniffing and the soft lull of the radio.

I knew Serena wasn't mad at me. I knew from the soft, sad smile she gave that she wasn't mad. That didn't mean I didn't still feel a bit guilty, though.

Serena worked hard with a job at a huge law firm further in the city. I knew her job could be stressful and it certainly wasn't made easier by having to leave early so she could attend to me and all my problems. I was just one more thing on her plate and I wished so deeply I could take back the nurse calling her to bring me home. I wish I had just walked home instead.

I had no doubt in my mind that she would say it wasn't a big deal. That she would understand why I needed to leave, needed her to come get me. That didn't lessen the guilt.

Even if she wasn't mad at me, she was clearly disappointed that she had to come. If not disappointed, then very clearly sad.

We had just pulled into the driveway when she finally turned to me and broke the silence, "Annie, what happened?"

"I-I...I was trying. I really was. I made it through first period. I didn't understand anything and I couldn't focus but I stayed. I was just trying to get to my second class and I- yeah." I sighed, tugging on the ends of my hair.

Serena frowned, "I'm sorry that happened. I'm so so sorry." She paused, sighing. "I will say that I'm also so proud of you for giving it a shot. You did the best you could today and that's all I asked for."

I smiled back at her weakly. Disappointment began to seep in. She could say she was proud all she wanted to but I knew deep down she was hoping for more. Maybe my best wasn't good enough today. Maybe I needed to actually try harder.

The rest of the morning, I mainly laid in bed and tried to nap off what happened. My head still ached a bit and my eyes stung from crying. I also had to shower the second I got home. I couldn't bare the feeling the burned itself into my skin any longer.

The nap did little to help, every time I closed my eyes, I felt like I was back in that hallway again. Choking, fainting, burning.

Before I knew it, it was already time to leave for my weekly therapist appointment.

I always dreaded it.

The way I would now eternally dread that hallway.

Wendy, my therapist, was a decently nice lady but there's not a single moment I can ever remember liking her. She certainly means well and I do think that she is knowledgable and trying her best to help me, but I have yet to feel like she actually understands my mind the way she thinks she does.

I hate the labels she always puts on me. It always manages to just make me feel broken and inadequate. I understand she's just trying to help but nothing she's said or done has ever felt like it's helping.

"I'll wait in the car like usual." Serena smiled at me as we pulled into the parking lot. She reached into the back seat and pulled out a book, sending me one last warm smile as I stepped out of the car.

I also hated the vibes of Wendy's office in general. Everything was an old brown color that made it hard to tell if it was on purpose or just from aging. The decor was so bland, it never ceased to make me feel sad and tired. The couches, at least, could be considered comfortable if you were able to overlook how dirty they had to be.

"Annie." Wendy's smile greeted me as she opened her office door.

Stepping to the side, she let me in. I passed her quickly and plopped down on my usual spot, brining my legs up to my chest instantly.

Wendy took a seat at her desk, pulling out her usual note pad and black ink pen before speaking, "So, you started school today?"

It sounded like a question but of course Wendy knew the answer. I just knew she was going to bring it up first thing since she was the reason I was even going in person to begin with. I was so close to convincing Serena to let me start with online school and get better on my own time when Wendy infused her 'professional opinion' on the topic. Serena of course grabbed at the chance and thus was the cause of my very horrible day.

I offered Wendy no response beyond a single sharp nod. I honestly had no interest in reliving what happened today but that of course was not going to matter much now because Wendy was going to do everything in her power to pull the admission out of me.

"Well...how did it go?" She pried again, staring at me so hard I felt like she was singlehandedly trying to reach the depths of my soul.

"It was fine." I stated. Obviously it wasn't fine but I really did not want to do this right now.

"Annie," Wendy sighed, "I'm not a dentist." She said, quirking a brow.

This was one of her favorite catch phrases. Always implying that getting an answer out of me was like pulling teeth, except dentists probably had an easier time with that. I know I didn't make it easy for her but I didn't think I could make it any clearer that I just don't want to talk about it.

"I passed out in the hallway." I gritted through my teeth, finally after several minutes of prolonged silence.

"Passed out? Oh my." Wendy's eyes brows shot up to her hairline. "And how did that come about?" She was scribbling away on her notepad now, glancing up occasionally as she wrote so as to prompt me to continue.

"I got anxious..." The answer felt too obvious, she should know this by now. I was one slip of the tongue away from adding 'duh' to the end of my sentence.

"Did you practice any of the techniques I taught you?" She asked, ever so slightly narrowing her eyes as he pen paused above the next line of her paper.

"Nope." I was digging my nails into my legs now, trying my best to control my irritation.

Wendy clicked her tongue but moved on, probably to come back to this after the lecture I knew I was going to receive shortly.

"What was the cause of the anxiety this time?" She asked.

She had said 'this time' with such an edge in her tone, I wanted to rip my hair out, screaming. That wouldn't go well if I didn't want to end up in the hospital, though.

"Boys. Small space. People touching me." I recited as quickly as I could, not wanting to dwell on any of them for too long. Just the brief remembrance of the feeling made my skin crawl in discomfort.

Androphobia.

Thats what Wendy calls it. An intense fear of men. Which was not too surprising after what had happened a few months ago. I couldn't stand them. All of them scared me. Their hands, their faces, their voices, their presence. I hated being in the same room as them as much as I hated breathing the same air as them.

Being stuck in such a small space. Being touched, hit, shoved by them in that hallway. That was terrifying.

This is why Wendy would never understand. She may have a diagnosis but all that meant to her was just a word on a piece of paper. A word that made her say certain things and tell me to make certain choices. That did not mean she could relate, understand, or even truly sympathize with the feelings that consumed my every waking moment.

Yet, I prayed that she never would have to understand because I wouldn't wish it upon my greatest enemy.

I left the office an hour later, feeling no better than I did when I had walked in.

I could never tell Serena this, though. It was something she hoped so deeply would help me get better. I couldn't bare the idea of crushing her with knowledge that I didn't think better was an option for me. Even if it was, I knew better wasn't going to come from Wendy.

Serena knew not to ask me how it went, I never really answered her. For as much as I didn't want to upset her, I also couldn't stomach the idea of lying either. Serena eventually let it go and stopped asking altogether.

Which is why I don't know what particularly came over me this time. The car ride had been just as silent as it had been earlier and yet I found myself wanting to break it. Wanting to let Serena know that I wasn't giving up effort even if I had given up hope.

"I'll try again." I said.

I hadn't realized how abruptly I'd spoken and how random just that sentence alone sounded. It had slipped from the confines of my mind.

"Going to school." I clarified, "I will try going to school again." I reiterated the complete sentence as it was meant in my mind.

Serena smiled so broadly, it warmed me up from head to toe.

"I was hoping you would say that." She grinned.

"I don't want to give up but I know it will take time."

"Baby steps. I believe in you just as confidently now as I did this morning. Just like I said earlier, you did great today. You just have to keep trying." Serena spoke.

"I will." I promised and I meant it.

AUTHOR'S NOTEHi friends!!! Thank you for choosing to read my book! If you've read it before, let me answer a few questions you might have if you haven't seen my message board. I am currently rewriting everything because even though I liked this book, I knew it wasn't my best work and I have been itching to make some adjustments. I hope you stick around and bare with me. I am feeling inspired and will try my best to stay consistent. I have already been updating the next few chapters so expect another one soon! Xoxo - Kat

4

S erena dropped me off just as early as she had the day before. This time not out of necessity but just so that I could avoid as many people as possible. The idea worked, there were even less students mulling about than there had been yesterday. It was only for that reason that I was able to pull myself out of the comfort of the car.

Serena yet again didn't hesitate to drive away the second I was out and the door was closed, leaving me all alone for the second time.

Regret burned in my chest. I could feel my fingernails on the brink of cutting through the first layer of the skin of my palms from how hard I was clenching my fist. I was doing this for Serena, I reminded myself. I had to repeat this mantra in my head several times before the feeling slowly ebbed away.

Releasing a shaky breath, I looked up the front steps unsurely. I didn't know where Knox was or if he'd even be here this early in the morning to begin with - probably not. I also didn't know if I should expect him to help me out again today or not. Technically the woman in the office never said how much he had to help me and considering the way yesterday went, I wouldn't be too surprised if he wanted to avoid me altogether now.

The only thing I really did know in this moment was that I absolutely did not want to walk into that hallway yet. The idea alone reignited the spark of regret along with the panic that was beginning to feel all too normal these days.

My legs wobbled slightly as I walked up the steps. It was as if my own body wanted to fight me from heading any closer to this place. I wasn't going inside yet, though. For now I was just content enough to sit outside on one of the benches near the main doors.

I was grateful to sit down, letting out a small sigh of relief at no longer standing on my unreliable legs.

It wasn't until I sat down that I realized it probably wasn't my smartest decision to wait in this exact spot. Being directly next to the main entrance of the school meant a lot of foot traffic, a lot of people walking right past me. Maybe even looking at me. It felt too late to move now. I couldn't gather enough strength to go somewhere else, not that I even knew where else I would go anyways.

So I sat in that same spot for who knows how long. I didn't move an inch save for the wringing of my hands together. Not even my eyes shifted, completely focused on the same spot of concrete in front of my feet.

Just because I couldn't see everyone passing by didn't meant I couldn't hear them. Every scuffling shoe, every conversation, every deep sigh just amplified my own terror. I thought I could manage ignoring everything but every time the door opened, my eye uncontrollably twitched.

I tried everything I could think of to distract myself. I dug my nails into my thighs, hoping the pain would make everyone else not seem as bad in comparison. I counted down from 100 for no reason other than my therapist had suggested it once - it didn't work. I even tried recanting my mantra but it didn't feel as significant as it had before I had sat down.

I could feel people looking me this time too. My skin prickled with discomfort at the thought.

I couldn't really blame them. I probably looked really odd sitting here with my head faced down to the ground and my body slightly shaking. I probably looked like a freak.

My eyes started filling with tears I couldn't control. I don't know why I thought I could do this again so soon. The day hadn't even truly started yet and I was already panicking. I should've known I wasn't ready to be here. Embarrassment coated me, making me redden.

A throat cleared in front me, two large shoes stepping into my previously undistributed view.

I jumped in my own skin at the sound. My head snapped up, connecting my tear-filled eyes with Knox's. He frowned down at me, almost certainly confused as to why I was already crying so soon. His eyes were questioning and he tilted his head ever so slightly.

My mouth dried, any words of greeting seemed impossible to manage.

"Good morning, Annie." Knox spoke, his voice just as gravely as the day before. His face seemed to be set in stone - thinking.

I swallowed harshly, nodding my head at him. The tears that had been starting to blur my vision slowly started subsiding. I felt shy now under his stare. Somehow knowing that at least some of his thoughts had to be about me, about the state of me, made me all the more self-conscious.

"The bell just rung." He stated, gesturing with his hand toward the front door.

I must not have heard it among all my internal panic. I drew in a sharp breath. I knew I would eventually have to face going to class but I couldn't help to wish that the moment would never come. I didn't move. Instead I stared blankly ahead, plagued with unease.

"I don't want to." I whispered, staring at the last few students scurrying through the doors.

Knox frowned again, staring down at me as he absorbed my words. I couldn't bare to look up at him again. I pulled at the ends of my hair, my knee starting to bounce of its own accord.

"Come." Knox broke the stiff air between us. His tone firm and his face completely serious.

I wanted to protest. He didn't understand what I was feeling right now. He had no right to tell me what to do, no right to ignore what I want. However, the fight I wanted to give died at the presence of his raised eyebrow.

I gulped, trying my best to suppress the oncoming embarrassment. I stood up trembling slightly. Knox looked like he was about to offer his hand but thought better of it.

"The hallway will be mostly empty now but hold the bottom of my shirt if you want to." Knox spoke again, his voice as soft as I could think it capable of being.

I nodded my head, ever so slightly reassured, before lightly taking hold of his t-shirt. My fingers anxiously fiddled with the stitching as we both started walking. I was grateful for the alternative to the backpack strap. It had been a good idea at the time but it also was easier for me to end up farther away from Knox - easier to get lost or hurt. Holding his shirt may have forced me to be much much closer to him, but it practically guaranteed more safety.

With the way people hurried to get out of his way, being closer to Knox in this hallway certainly felt like a good thing.

Knox had been right. The hallways held very few lingering students which allowed us to walk completely freely. The calm quiet of classes being in session allowed me to relax my shoulders as we walked.

I hadn't been paying attention to where we were going until we reached the familiar door of the front office. Only once we were inside did I feel comfortable enough to let go of his shirt.

Knox walked straight up the desk where the same woman as yesterday sat. I lingered closely behind him, peaking over his shoulder at the woman in slight confusion as to why we had come in here again so soon.

"Linda." Knox drew her attention, redirecting her usual beaming smile towards us.

"What can I do for you, Knox?" Her eyes twinkled as she spotted me behind him.

"I need Annie's schedule like mine." He all but demanded.

"Oh?" Her smile didn't falter. "And why is that?"

"You asked me to show Annie around. I can't do that and get to all of my classes at the same time." His tone was unwavering, as if he was daring Linda to argue with him.

I shifted on my feet, looking between the two of them as the spoke. It seems my presence was quickly forgotten. All I could think about was the fact that I was so glad that Knox's intensive stare and unwavering tone was not directed at me. Even if Linda did seem to be handling it well.

"Oh, well that certainly isn't good, is it? Well, if you can't do it, Knox, maybe I could find someone on the welcoming committee to take over. They are better trained for this kind of thing anyways." Linda tilted her head, matching Knox's challenge.

"That's not necessary." Knox practically grit out.

I bit my lip, growing increasingly more uncomfortable with his display of frustration.

"You'd have to get a meeting with her counselor in order to make any class changes. You know that already, Knox."

"Linda," Knox took a deep breath. "We both know that you are able to change it without a counselor. You asked me to help Annie and I'm doing it."

Linda considered Knox's words for several tense seconds. It seemed he finally said something that Linda had wanted to hear because she started typing away at her computer again, another smile tugging at the corners of her mouth.

"Fine, but don't tell Principle Hendrick." She said.

Five minutes later, Linda slid a new copy of my schedule across the counter. Knox snatched it off the counter before I could even make any move to grab it. He stuffed it in his back pocket before letting out a gruff 'thank you' and turning away to leave.

My mouth parted and eyes widened, having to quickly latch back onto him as he started walking out. I wasn't sure whether I was supposed to feel relieved about his guaranteed continued presence or not but it seemed like I wasn't getting much choice in the matter regardless.

The bell seemed to have rung again without my notice or maybe it just doesn't ring in the office. Either way, the hall was back to how I had experienced it yesterday. Knox seemed to think better of trying to fight our way through like last time and instead we stood in the alcove of the office door, waiting for it to clear out a bit more before walking again.

There were still a lot of students hurrying by but once the bulk of them had gone down, Knox started walking with me still almost in step with him.

He weaved us through with a lot more ease this time. Not a single person glanced our direction nor did I find myself being a jostled a single time. I almost relished in being able to hide slightly behind Knox's shoulder. The entire experience had been so difference from the last; so much so that I even found myself thinking that maybe this boy - just this one - wasn't so bad after all.

5

- -

F rom the near lack of empty desks in the classroom, it appeared that Knox and I were that last few to show up. Not surprising considering our absence of hurry after leaving the office. Normally I'd be worried about being some of the last to show up - worried about all the eyes that would surly dart to me.

That worry didn't come though, and apparently there was no reason for it to.

Even though Knox and I had arrived on the brink of being late, the rest of the class were still taking to their seats, fussing with their notebooks and pencils and laptops, and from the noise encasing the room, still in the midsts of conversation. Not a single glance could be spared in our direction.

Knox didn't pause in the doorway for longer than a split second before veering off to the back of the room with me still being tugged along with him. There were only two seats left in the back row - two seats that shared the same table just as it was for every other table in the classroom.

I gulped, licking my dry lips as my eyes flitted around the room. I had yet to actually see my new schedule, Knox having taken it right away even though he already knew what it was as it had now matched his own. The desks gave me some clue as to what the class was but I hadn't truly known until my eyes found the papers that hung all around the room - Art.

Reaching the two seats, Knox took the aisle which left me the chair directly next to the wall. Now sitting down, I released a tense breath. Nobody to my right, only Knox to my left, and a girl in front of me. The tight grip of my chest eased, quickly being replaced with the hope that maybe I could actually focus this time around.

I wiped my sweaty palms off on my skirt just as my new teacher took to gathering our attention.

"Good morning, all. Like I told you yesterday, since it is only the first week of school, we will not be starting any projects as of yet..." she paused, giving a knowing smile before continuing. "That doesn't mean we won't be working, of course. New to practicing art or not, I want you all to get comfortable with allowing your mind to take creative reign."

I chewed on the bottom lip, my leg bouncing as I listened. I was not particularly "new to art" as she had phrased it but that didn't mean I was very skilled at art either. I enjoyed painting the most out of any other medium - finding the vivid colors, textures, and softness of the stroke of a paint brush to be soothing.

I wasn't specifically good at painting anything to a realistic degree. I more so enjoyed a mild interpretation of the basic elements. I hadn't found the inspiration to paint in months though. Not after what had happened.

I almost jerked in my seat, surprised once my teacher's voice found my ears again, "Each of you should have a blank piece of paper on the desk in front of you and I trust you all brought your own pencil to use. If you did not, I do have some spares that I would like back before you leave. We'll be doing this for the rest of class and you are to finish the assignment for homework.

Don't worry about it being perfect, I just want to measure where each of you are at individually. Go ahead and start." She smiled before turning around to sit back down at her own desk.

I looked around the room and saw everyone either digging in their backpacks for a pencil or already reaching for their paper. My face blanched, embarrassed I had zone out long enough to almost entirely miss what we were supposed to be drawing in the first place.

I glanced over at Knox only to find him already looking at me, his body slightly turned slightly in my direction with a pencil already in his grasp. The slight pull of a knowing smile on his lips told me he must have understood the look of confusion on my face - he was just waiting for me to ask.

"W-what are we drawing?" I asked, my voice just above a whisper.

"A portrait of each other." Knox replied without hesitation, his head tilting to the side as he continued to study my face.

My lips parted in an 'o' as I sucked in a sharp breath. Already being this close to Knox and in his constant presence since arriving at school had felt like enough of a challenge. But to have him staring - no, studying my face so as to recreate it on his paper? That felt way more intimate than holding on to the lining of his t-shirt.

"Don't wanna draw me, Annie?" Knox quirked a brow, almost challenging me.

My heart leaped to my throat, almost making me choke on the air I couldn't breath. Knox was still a boy. An intimidating boy who had hands that could easily hurt me - hands that could crush me in an instant. And yet, he also had a heart that had only chosen to help me so far.

I would remain wary but being wary of him didn't mean not returning the kindness he had only been showing me so far.

"N-no. I mean -" I shook my head and sighed, attempting to start my sentence over. "I mean I have no problem drawing you." I looked down at my paper, trying to fight the blush that was threatening to overtake my face.

"Good cause it'd be real mean if you didn't want to draw me." Knox said, a ghost of a smile twitching at the corners of his mouth.

"Mean?" My eyes snapped back to his as I furrowed my brow in confusion.

"Exactly. Wouldn't wanna break my heart, would you, Annie?" Knox asked, his eyes twinkling with mischief.

I shook my head, swallowing hard.

"Good girl." Knox praised lowly.

My eyes widened and I turned back to my blank paper, trying to distract myself from the tingle that shot down my spine. Knox's soft chuckle filled my ears, sending the same sensation shooting through my body that I would pretend to ignore yet again.

The rest of the class consisted of silent drawing. Knox studying my face far more than I was willing to study his. I could only bring myself to peek at him for a handful of seconds at a time, half of which lasted only as long as it took him to look back at me again, leaving me unable to bare the eye contact.

The bell ringing had me quickly stuffing the paper and my pencil back in my bag and standing up to latch onto Knox once again.

I felt more stiff this time, the moment between us still hung awkwardly in the air. Maybe Knox didn't feel it since he didn't bother to acknowledge it, but I sure felt it. Now with his back to me, I found my eyes looking over him far more often than they had during the entire class period.

I again was not sure what our next class was or even where we were going. We had waited, like last time, until most of the hallway had cleared out before we made our way.

My head was in the clouds, lost too deep in thought. My eyes were shifting back and forth between Knox's back and the hallway in front of us. I was probably looking between the two too quickly. Maybe I should've been looking at my feet instead - in fact, I know that's exactly what I should have been doing.

Instead, my untied shoe went unnoticed just long enough that I tripped right over it. I stumbled, letting go of the hem of Knox's shirt before landing right in the middle of the hallway on my hands and knees. I whimpered, a bunch of my hair falling in front of my face from the impact.

Tears were already completely clouding my vision when two hands found their way under my arms, lifting me back up and onto my feet.

I slightly stumbled again, my knees gone weak from hitting the hard ground. I was pulled into a strong chest, one arm wrapping around my waist while the palm of a hand held my head against their chest.

Knox's voice met my ears with a soothing, gentle 'shh.' I could feel myself shaking with quiet cries. My bottom lip wobbled uncontrollably as I pulled my head back and looked at Knox's blurry outline.

"I wanna go home." I whined, beginning to hiccup as I tried to repress the sobs that threatened to come out.

"I know, baby. Let's get you home." Knox whispered, trying his best the wipe the tears coating my cheeks with the pad of his thumb.

Serena picked me up from the office an hour later. Knox waited in the seat next to mine the entire time, his arm resting over the top of my chair. Occasionally he paused the gentle twirling of a few strands of my hair, leaning over to whisper words of comfort - mainly whenever he noticed my eyes getting misty again.

Serena drove me home in silence just like the day before, only less tense. I had made it farther than yesterday and she made sure to reassure that she was proud of me before she left to go back to work - unable to work from home a second day out of the week.

I immediately changed into pajamas and wrapped myself in blankets on the couch, turning on my comfort movie, Lilo and Stitch, in order to calm myself down. I was still sniffling an hour and 25 minutes later when the credits were rolling and I realized I hadn't been paying a lick of attention the entire time.

The sting of my knees had been barely noticeable now and there weren't any visible scrapes. It was more so the mortification of not only the fact that I fell, but that I fell in the middle of the hallway and only steps behind Knox. Not that I thought he was really judging me and not that I should have cared regardless but it was hard to pretend not to care.

I gripped my hair at the roots, tears of frustration surfacing again. I was so sick and tired of crying all the time. I was sick and tired of constantly letting everything get to me. And yet, I couldn't stop it either.

Dropping my hands, I tried to calm my breathing. Looking at the now black screen of the tv, I thought back to the boy who had done nothing but help me. The boy who not only made sure he could get me to my classes safely, but also who witness multiple of my breakdowns. Not only witnessed these breakdowns but who helped me get through them instead of making fun of me.

Knox may have not wanted my thanks but I couldn't allow myself to not express my gratitude in some way.

Looking to my right, mind and heart still racing, I tossed my blanket aside and entered the kitchen with my mind made up.

6

I waited on the same bench next to the main doors as I had yesterday morning. Only this time I wasn't staring down at my feet. I was looking around, wringing my hands together anxiously as I waited for Knox. My entire mind so consumed with looking for him, I paid no attention to the many people, many boys, passing me with curious looks.

The palms of my hands felt clammy from nervous sweat. My foot couldn't stop shaking beneath me. And my eyes darted all around me, probably closely resembling some kind of tweaker.

By the time I saw him finally strolling up the steps, eyes set on me, the bell signaling first period rang through the air. Leaving me with no time to thank him yet.

I couldn't help the disappointment that was already filling my veins. I had been anxiously awaiting this moment since last night. I had barely been able to sleep because of how much I couldn't stop thinking about it, desperate to know whether or not Knox would like what I made him. I probably should feel naive and stupid for how much I wanted his approval on this gift to the point of total consumption.

Knox approached me and wordlessly held out his hand for me which I unconsciously took hold of. I hadn't even realized what I had done until he was already tugging me alone with him through the hall.

His hand was rough with callouses and slightly sweaty, or maybe that was my hand, and it completely engulfed my own. My heart was beating so fast, I was afraid he would either hear it or it would burst out of me and land before us on the shiny hall tiles. I waited for the panic to set in, waited for the tight feeling in my throat and chest.

It only squeezed for a second before releasing.

We walked into first period seconds before the late bell rung. This was not like how we had walked into art. Looking at the walls, I guessed English, before Knox all but dragged me to two seats in the back again. All around the room, I felt curious eyes roaming over me. Even the teacher still sitting at his desk gave Knox and I a scathing look.

My guess about English was correct.

Our teacher started talking the second Knox and I sat down and didn't stop talking the entire period. It became excruciatingly hard to focus. My mind reeling with thoughts of giving Knox my 'thank you' present, my skin burning with the knowledge that I'd held his hand, and the sideways looks the people in the surrounding seats kept giving me.

My mind felt foggy, clouded with my self-consciousness. I yet again found myself unable to sit still. I felt itchy from the feeling of everyone's stare touching me. I scratched my knee, then shoulder, then neck, tucked my hair behind my ear, untucked it, itched my elbow, repeat.

I wanted to scratch everybody's eyes out and watch them bleed for the consequences of their judgement upon me. I needed to get out of this stuffy room before I actually imploded. Maybe then Wendy would see that this was too soon, that I hadn't been ready for this challenge after all.

I had only jotted down two bullet points about anything my teacher said before the bell rang and everyone started filing out.

Knox yet again held my hand the entire walk to art which only managed to make my mind spiral faster. My face was flushed and my entire body felt sweaty. The bemused look Knox shot my way only told me that I must have looked a panicked mess by the time we took our seats.

"Okay, everyone. Take out your drawings from last class. Remember that it doesn't have to be perfect, as long as you drew something and it's clear you tried, I will be happy." Our teacher spoke.

My head snapped to look at Knox stifling a grin. 'As long you draw something.' My breathing shallowed. Time seemed to slow down as I absorbed her words. He tricked me. He tricked me into drawing him because he knew I wasn't paying attention - he knew I would do it.

Heat flooded my face, if I was flushed before it was nothing compared to now. My hands shook unsteadily as I pulled out my paper, my attempted rendering of the boy inches away from me.

I had barely set it down when his hand snatched it, pulling it in front of him, eyes darting all over the page - taking it all in. I wanted to protest, wanted to snatch it back, but I was already too embarrassed and it was a fight I didn't think I would win - a fight I didn't have the energy for.

The smile that he held was very different from the one moments before, this was one was far less mischievous - far more easy and real. He slid the paper back in front of me, eyes filled with an emotion I couldn't place.

I looked down at my drawing. It wasn't my best work. I wasn't nearly as good with a pen or pencil as I was with a paint brush, but I would say that I tried a lot harder with this than I did with anything I had ever painted before. I still didn't think I got it perfect, but clearly my model was happy enough so I was grateful not to have insulted him.

An hour and another class later, the bell signaled lunch. I was grateful that it was Friday, all of our Friday's were half days. It made it feel like I was making a lot more progress getting through the day than I had been able to previously and in a way, I was making a lot more progress. I had already made it to lunch time - something I hadn't been able to do before now. That didn't make the idea any less daunting.

I was holding onto the seam of Knox's shirt yet again. I don't know if I would have been able to stomach the cafeteria while holding his hand, my body would be too wired. I was also already significantly warn out from the rollercoaster of emotions I had been feeling since the moment I stepped foot on campus.

We stood in line, Knox holding the tray and loading it up for us the whole way through. I just stood silently, still holding on next to him. I had my back to the countless tables that filled the room. I knew if I so much as glanced at them, I would be panicking far more than just looking at the food Knox put on the tray.

I didn't release a breath until we were out the doors of the cafeteria, heading towards the grassy fields behind the school.

Knox led us to a picnic table shaded under a lone tree near the football field. A few people sat sprawled in the lawn, even more people speckled around the bleachers. There were a few more tables in the sun a few yards away that had some stray students studying or working on homework.

I was surprised this table wasn't taken but was grateful nonetheless.

Setting down the tray, Knox sat down across from me. He slid me a slice of pizza before digging into his own. We ate in silence as I looked out at all the people around us. It was nice to be out in the fresh air. After spending all morning inside stuffy, suffocating classrooms, unable to focus, it was relieving to sit here without so much worry.

To sit somewhere I felt like I could breath deeply again.

I could feel Knox looking at me. Yet, for some reason, it wasn't bothering me. It made me a bit nervous, of course, but I didn't feel anxious in the way I felt with other people's stares.

I guess, in a way, I was grateful it was Knox looking at me rather than anyone else. At least I couldn't feel any judgement radiating off of him - no feelings of malintent.

I forced down my last bite, dusting my hands off before I was able to meet his eyes. I had become so caught up in the confusion of the morning that I had completely forgot what I had gone into this day planning to do.

I dug around in my backpack for a second before my fingers clasped onto the tupperware container that had been bulking up my bag all day. I slid the container of chocolate chip cookies across the table, biting my cheek in fear he wouldn't like them.

"What's this?" Knox asked, his mouth half full of pizza.

"Cookies." I replied, licking my perpetually dry lips.

He nearly rolled his eyes, "Yeah, but why?"

I cleared my throat, "I made them for you - to say thank you."

Knox stared at me blankly, swallowing the bite he had taken from his pizza.

"I don't need you to thank me." He said.

"I -" I paused, frowning. I knew he had said this before but couldn't he understand what he was doing for me - what he had already done for me. The change he was making in my life was something I absolutely needed to thank, something I couldn't find the words to express.

Silence filled the air between us as he watched me struggling to search for the words to express my gratitude. Finally sparing me, he pulled off the lid and reached for a cookie. I waited breathless for a reaction once he bit into it. I wasn't the best baker but I had baked these cookies from scratch, completely from the heart.

He finished the cookie before reaching for another one. I let out my breath, I suppose that one action would have to be enough of a reaction for me as he still spoke no words.

By the time lunch was over, most of the cookies were gone and before Knox led me to our next class, he leaned down and whispered a gruff 'thank you' in my ear.

7

The final bell was the most relieving noise I had heard all day.

Watching as everyone quickly shuffled out of our last class felt like a big weight had been lifted off my shoulders. I was quite honestly surprised I had managed to make it through the entire day - even if we had gotten out earlier than a normal school day. I was certain Serena would be even more surprised than I was and most certainly relieved too.

I was slow in gathering my things together. I willed my hands not to shake as Knox waited, his eyes watchful as he stood at the desk next to me.

Walking through the hallway at the end of the day was undoubtably the best time. Everyone was in such a rush to leave that if you just meandered enough in the back, you were among very few stragglers. So few, I didn't even feel a need to hold onto Knox in anyway. Apparently I was wiling to make leaps and bounds today. Now they just had to stick.

The gentle breeze of the fresh outside air tickled my nose and I was more than happy to breath it in. Even most of the traffic had already cleared out. I hadn't realized I was being so slow but it seemed to be paying off for me.

Stopping at the bottom of the steps, I turned to face Knox. I was planning to walk home since Serena would still be working for a few more hours. Before I could say a word of goodbye, Knox was already speaking.

"Come get Ice Cream with me." He said in more of a demand than a question.

"Ice Cream?" I asked, quirking my head to the side.

We stared at each other for several silent moments, nothing but the breeze passing between us.

"C'mon." He turned and started walking again before I could truly answer one way or the other.

I supposed it didn't really matter. I wanted to go regardless. Why would anyway ever say no to the opportunity of ice cream anyways? I certainly couldn't do that.

Knox led me to his car, opening the door so I could clamber in. As we rode, only the low rumble of his music filled the air around us. After being surrounded by never ending loud noise all day, I had to say that this change was welcomed.

We pulled up to a parlor I had yet to see before. It was super cute in a classic mom-and-pop type of way. Their logo was a little pink cow sitting and eating a giant cone of ice cream. For a mascot, it was utterly adorable.

Cool air washed over us the second we stepped inside making me shiver slightly. My eyes darted all around. While and pink checkered tiles filled the floor and matched the check-out counter. There were several booths littered around the perimeter of the space, each seat as bubble gum pink as the next.

A little pink bobble head of their mascot sat atop the cash register. My lips quirked at the sight.

"Any idea what you want?" Knox's voice brought me out of my trance.

I looked up at the menu above the counter. Growing up, I'd only gone to an ice cream shop maybe once and I certainly never lived in a house that had any waiting for me in the freezer. I couldn't even remember any flavor of ice cream I've tried before.

"What do you normally get?" I asked softly.

Hopefully my question came off as if I was more of an adventurous foodie than a girl who hadn't really experienced something as simple as ice cream before. Knox didn't seem to think twice about it thankfully.

"Vanilla." Knox shrugged, looking back down at me.

Vanilla was always a safe option. I'd had enough sweets to know that much. It was just as safe as getting chocolate but glancing a the menu one more time, I still felt completely unsure. I was seconds away from just saying I'd get the same thing as him when he spoke again.

"Do you want me to pick for you?" He asked.

I chewed on my lip - a nervous habit I needed to break - before nodding my head 'yes.'

Stepping up the counter, Knox nodded his head at the cashier who had asked if we were ready, "Yeah, we'll have one scoop vanilla in a cone and another strawberry swirl also in a cone."

I was about the reach for the money I kept wedged between my phone case but Knox didn't bat an eye as he paid for it. The cashier handed over the cones seconds later, Knox handing me mine immediately.

"Thank you." I whispered as we sat at a booth in the corner.

There were a few other people in the other booths. There was what appeared to be a father and his two sons and then another couple of girls our age. Thankfully neither party was too close to our booth.

"Don't worry about it." Knox winked, beginning to eat his ice cream.

I was grateful that he had ordered for me. The first bite I took was heavenly, nearly making my tastebuds sing. Now I knew for future reference that strawberry swirl needed to be my go-to.

Knox unsurprisingly finished before me.

"Like it?" He asked.

I nodded, licking my lips.

"This is my new favorite." I admitted, my voice muffled by the next bite I took.

Knox smiled through a short, breathy laugh.

"Thank you, Knox." I said, again after finishing my cone.

"Annie, you really need to stop thanking me." He sighed, leaning back with his arms crossed.

"I can't help it." I whispered, frowning.

My words hung in the air for a few seconds. I had to admit that silences like these weren't as uncomfortable with Knox. I wasn't a huge talker and it was clear Knox wasn't either. I suppose it wouldn't have been a big deal for either of us to just let the silence go forever.

That was until I realized that I didn't actually want to stay silent around him. If we were going to be friends, I needed to start getting used to actually talking to him.

"Why'd you lie about the drawing assignment?" I asked. My tone far more accusing than I meant it to be. It wasn't as if I was truly upset about the situation at all, I was simply curious why he chose to lie in the first place. Even then, it probably wasn't best first choice of conversation topic.

Luckily Knox just threw his head back and laughed.

"I didn't lie to you." He chuckled.

"Yes, you did. You told me that we had to draw each other." I frowned.

He was smirking again, "No. You asked what we specifically were going to draw and I decided for us. You didn't ask me what she actually assigned."

I mulled over his semantics, furrowing my brows further.

"I thought that my true question was understandable enough." I argued, grumbling.

"You didn't seem to be complaining." Knox rolled his eyes playfully, a teasing smile playing at the corners of his mouth.

My cheeks reddened. Trying to play off his words, I sighed. Technically could have been clearer and there were far worse things to lie about than just what to draw for an art class. I was just more embarrassed that he had tricked me than anything else.

Another beat of silence passed between us before he leaned forward again, speaking, "Let me see your phone."

He extended the palm of his hand, looking at me expectantly. His demand was soft but it was a demand nonetheless. I furrowed my brows in confusion but placed it in his waiting palm anyways.

"No password?" He raised an eyebrow, glancing at me briefly before returning his focus to my screen.

I shook my head. I hadn't had a phone of my own for very long. Serena had bought it for me when I first arrived at her house. Being welcomed into her home was gift enough for me, the phone had become an unexpected bonus. I didn't bother putting a password on it because I guess I didn't really see a reason to. I was hardly on it and I didn't really keep anything personal on it.

"What're you doing?" I finally asked. I mentally scolded myself, I probably should have asked before handing it over to begin with.

"Texting myself." Knox replied cooly.

"Why?" I was growing even more confused.

"So I have your number." He answered matter-of-factly.

"Oh..." I said, his answer feeling obvious now that he said it. "Does that mean we're friends now?" I asked, warmth flooding my chest.

Knox looked up at me, his fingers hovering over my screen. His eyes darkened and twinkled with an emotion I either couldn't place or didn't understand.

"I'll take whatever you give me, Annie." Knox said, shifting his eyes back to my phone.

8

S un filtered in through an open sliver of my curtains, beaming me in the eye the next morning. I had been awake for a while, opting to stay in bed, unmoving instead of bothering to get up and start a day that held no plans.

Knox had driven me home right after the ice cream parlor and thats what I laid thinking about now. I hadn't truly expected him to be so nice to me.

No boy had ever really been that nice to me. Not a single boy other than ... not that it mattered now as it didn't end well anyways. Knox was nice to me though. He even agreed to be my friend and lord knew I had no others I'd never been good at making friends. I moved houses too much for too long. I didn't stick around long enough to make a lasting impression on anyone. I didn't even really learn the skill of keeping friends - bonding like that.

I learned to form quick attachments - even if they weren't always the best or healthiest for me.

I rolled over to face away from the sun beaming at me. I closed my eyes for a second, taking a deep, steady breath. In through my nose and out through my mouth.

I hated remembering my childhood. I was tired of reflecting on it. I spent too much time in my own mind, and I didn't want to waste my Saturday thinking about every bad thing that happened in my life.

Kicking my legs over the side of my bed, I stretched out my arms far above my head.

I may have slept in a few hours later than usual but I still felt sleepy. I had gone to bed quite a bit later than intended. After Knox had dropped me off at home, Serena and I spent the night zoned into our favorite reality tv show - binge watching it well into the night. Once we started, it felt impossible to stop, and so we didn't.

Deciding to get a head start on my homework, I pulled out my binder from my backpack and started sorting through all the papers I had collected throughout the week. There wasn't that much to do but I wanted to get it out of the way before I did anything else so that I could truly just focus on relaxing.

It was noon by the time I had finished. Serena had popped her head in an hour ago, bringing me a sandwich and fresh lemonade. She truly was the kindest person and I was immensely grateful for her.

She did have to leave right after that though as she had a bunch of work she still needed to catch up on. I admittedly felt pretty bad about that considering I made her leave work early multiple times this week. And no matter much she tried to reassure me that it wasn't my fault, it was hard not to feel like I was at least partially to blame.

"It's a beautiful day, Annie. Why don't you go to the park, walk in the sun and get some fresh air." She had suggested before she left.

And looking past my now open curtains through my window, she had been right. It really was a beautiful day and now that I was done with my work, I couldn't see a reason not to go outside.

The only thing was that I knew I didn't want to go alone.

Pulling out my phone, I texted the only person's number - besides Serena - that I had in my contact list.

Knox replied back in an instant, agreeing to meet me there.

With my heart racing, I rushed to pull on one of my favorite baby-blue sun dresses. It was still summer time and if I wore anything else, I knew I'd be sweating ridiculously. Slipping on some white sandals, I headed out the door.

The park was only a couple blocks from my house. A short, easy walk with just enough nature along the way that it felt thoroughly enjoyable.

The nearer I got, the more jittery I could feel myself getting. The antici-pation of seeing Knox was for some reason affecting me differently today. I was starting to get used to seeing his face not only everyday but at almost every moment throughout as well. It was already beginning to feel weird getting this far in the day without seeing him.

I spotted him leaning against his car, parked under a giant shaded oak.

He was looking down at his phone, typing away. He hadn't noticed me until I was a couple steps away, his eyes then burning into mine.

"Hi." I breathed, smiling as I stopped before him.

The corner of his mouth twitched as he shoved his phone back in his pocket.

"I brought a blanket." Knox said, turning around to open his back seat and pulling out a yellow checkered picnic blanket.

"Oh, perfect. Thank you." I gushed, smiling brighter now.

I hadn't really had a plan when I invited him here with me so I was grateful that at least he had thought of something.

Together we walked out through the grass, it's length tickling my ankles. Dandelions were growing sporadically and it was becoming a struggle to resist picking one.

Knox laid out the blanket under another tree, farther away from the parking lot and the playground which was active with small children. He laid down before me, looking back up at me expectantly to which I followed by plopping down next to him.

It was if he could tell that another 'thank you' was on the very tip of my tongue, threatening to slip out, because after prolonged moments of silence, Knox finally broke it.

"I used to play soccer on this field as a kid." He said, glancing slightly behind his shoulder.

I grinned, "That's a cute memory to have."

Knox shrugged, deciding to move on. "You keep staring down the dandelions. They'll all shrivel up if you look at them any harder." He joked.

I blushed, not realizing I had made myself so obvious.

"The first place I lived had a million dandelions in the cracks of the sidewalk leading up to the house. My favorite pass time was making wishes on them." I paused, smiling down at my hands. "There were almost none left by the time I moved away. I had picked them so much, most of them stopped growing back."

"What'd you used to wish for?" Knox asked curiously.

A frown tugged at the corner of my mouth as I mulled over my words, searching for the best way to put it.

"That every step would be better than the last." I finally settled on.

Knox picked a dandelion that had been near the edge of the blanket before twirling it between his fingers. Shifting his eyes from the dandelion to me, he held it up in front of my lips. I glanced between him and the flower before blowing on it, making a new wish.

"What'd you wish for now?" He asked, throwing away the stem.

"I can't tell you. It's a secret." I laughed.

Knox snorted at my words, rolling his eyes.

We didn't stay at the park for too long. Eventually it had become unbearably hot outside, the air thick and still from the lack of breeze. Slick with sweat and growing tired and sluggish, we both decided it was time to leave.

Walking back to Knox's car was slow, our pace reflecting the feel of the heat. I was still grateful to have spent this time here with him regardless of the heat though. It felt like now his shell was starting to crack and I honestly felt myself growing far more comfortable in his presence than I would have ever expected. I was become really glad to be his friend.

Knox had offered to drive me home to which I couldn't refuse. That little bit of A/C was an irresistible thought, especially when the alternative was walking several blocks.

Maybe it was the heat exhaustion, maybe it was genuine curiosity, or it could have even been a bad slip of the tongue but on the ride back I found myself breaking our comfortable silence.

"Have you ever had a girlfriend?" I asked, a blush quickly rising at my words.

Knox chuckled slight, taken a bit by surprise.

"Yeah..." He laughed, "a couple but never serious." He answered nonchalantly.

The desire to smack myself in the head became very strong. Of course he's had girlfriends before. What kind of question was that? A guy like Knox was bound to have a few. I should have expected that. I was embarrassed I even felt the need to ask.

"Oh, right." I mumbled, turning my head to look out the window. "You don't want to know if I've ever had a boyfriend?" I asked, the words yet again tumbling out of me. This was a nightmare. It had to be heat stroke at this point, there couldn't be any other excuse.

I watched as Knox's eyebrows rose quickly, even more taken aback than before. He seemed to be trying his best to suppress the amusement that wanted to overtake his face and he was not being very successful.

"Well, my innocent little Annie, have you ever had a boyfriend before?" He asked to appease me.

Blood rushed to my face even faster. Obviously he knew the answer. It was obvious even in the way he had phrased the question. I don't know why I was forcing him to ask me when I didn't actually want to admit it to him now. I wish I would have swallowed my words.

"No." I forced out quietly.

"Do you want one?" Knox pressed, fully grinning now.

"I don't know." My cheeks burned with the regret of bringing up this entire conversation.

"You don't know?" He questioned again.

My embarrassment was turning into anger which quickly turned into sorrow.

"Stop teasing me." I whined, tears burning at the back of my eyes from frustration.

I was completely mortified, the feeling seeping out of my every pore. I couldn't stand this conversation any longer. Grateful my house was in view, I was desperate to escape the car.

"I'm not teasing you, Annie." Knox said, his tone growing more serious as he realized the state of my emotions. "Annie, baby, don't cry. I wasn't trying to upset you." He said, pulling up to the curb of my house and parking.

I wiped at my eyes, doing my best to stifle my cries.

"I'm sorry." I whispered, hiccuping slightly.

"No, I'm sorry. I was being an ass. Forgive me, please?" Knox asked, leaning closer as he brushed away my stray tears.

I nodded an 'okay', looking at him through my wet lashes before bidding him 'goodbye' and stepping out the car to head into my house.

9

"Ouch." I whispered, bringing my freshly pricked thumb to my lips to suck off the bead of blood that had begun to form. I silently cursed myself for agreeing to help Serena in the garden this morning. Neither of us had particularly green thumbs but Serena had decided three weeks ago that she wanted to give gardening a shot. Claiming to want a new, quiet activity that would get us both outside to be at peace with nature.

The only issue being that nature wasn't exactly at peace with me.

Of course the flower Serena wanted to have the most was a classic rose. Only she wasn't the one who now had to plant them, instead delegating that task to me.

I didn't come out here with intention of gardening myself, I just wanted to say 'good morning' since I was up. Obviously things didn't work out my way. Serena was so enthused I had come out here to help that I didn't have the heart to correct her.

I sat back on my heals, wiping the sweat off my brow. The action no doubt only managing to spread more dirt around my face.

We had been out here for hours now, the sun out in full effect. The summer season was supposed to be nearing its end but apparently mother nature had yet to get the memo.

I grimaced down at the flower before me. I couldn't understand why we were planting these now, with autumn and then winter just around the corner. Regardless I would do what would make Serena happy without arguing.

I guess it was good to have the distraction after yesterday.

Knox was beginning to consume my mind. The time we spent at the park was the most peaceful I've felt in a long time - certainly more peaceful than I felt gardening at this moment. Even our conversation in the car couldn't take away from the enjoyment I felt.

Truly I wasn't upset about that conversation, either.

If anything, I was mainly embarrassed. The fact that I had even let myself ask him those questions were humiliating enough. So much so that the thought of facing him again tomorrow made my skin heat up.

"What do you say we call it a day and I make us some lemonade?" Serena called from a few planters away.

I nodded as enthusiastically as the heat exhaustion would allow me to.

"I'm going to shower." I breathed, dragging myself to my feet.

Serena nodded her head, only steps behind me as I headed inside.

I sighed, letting myself fall onto my bed with my arms spread wide, landing on my stomach. The coolness of my now wet hair almost making me flinch as it came to rest against my still sun-warmed skin. This feeling after my shower had made gardening all morning well worth it. Maybe Serena wasn't so wrong about needing that peaceful outside activity after all.

The soft chime of my phone quickly drew my attention.

I sat up, staring at my phone where it had rested on my nightstand all morning. I could feel my heart rate picking up already. Only two people had my phone number and Serena certainly had no reason to text when her shouts could easily be heard by me from the down stairs.

Snatching it off my nightstand, my breathing hitched as Knox's name flashed on my screen.

"You busy?" He asked.

My fingers tingled like the buzz of tv static as I replied 'no.'

"I'm picking you up." He said.

It wasn't a question but I liked the text message as confirmation anyways. Letting out a steady breath, I rushed to my closet to start getting dressed. Blindly grabbing the first things I touched, I ended up in a white knitted tank top and my favorite pair of jean shorts. Slipping my feet into my normal white sneakers, I gave my hair one more quick brush.

Every movement I made was frantic with a slight jerk. My nerves were skyrocketing and not knowing how long Knox would take to get here was setting me on edge.

I scrambled down the stairs. My rush to the kitchen was met with Serena's confusion.

"What's got you in such a rush?" She asked, drinking a glass of the lemonade she promised to make.

"I-uh I'm going out." I said hurriedly. I hadn't told Serena about how I had made a friend. Even if I knew she would be excited for me, I also knew she'd make it a thing and that was something I could say for certain that I didn't want. It'd only embarrass me further to know that me making a friend could be so shocking. Especially if Serena caught a glimpse of who my friend actually is. Knox being my friend would send a shock wave through Serena.

"Don't wait up for me. I don't know when I'll be back." I rushed to fill the silence, not wanting to give Serena the time to follow up with questions.

I spun on my heel, nearly jogging for the front door. A cool breath of relief passed my lips as the door shut behind me. My eyes flitted to the car now pulling up against the curb.

"Hi." I nearly whispered as I stepped into the car, pulling on my seatbelt.

Knox sent a ghost of a smile in my direction as he pulled back out onto the street.

"Where are we going?" I asked, not breaking my gaze out the window.

"My friend's house." He answered cooly, not sparing me a glance.

I turned to look at him with furrowed brows, my body shifting in my seat uneasily. He never mentioned anything about bringing me to meet anyone, I was hoping it would just be him and I like normal. I'm sure his friends had to be decent people but the idea of who Knox could possibly surround himself with was thoroughly intriguing.

"Why?" I hesitated, "I mean, why are you bringing me along?"

Knox looked my way for only a second before his eyes were back on the road. "Cause I want to and I can." He said, almost scoffing at my question. "Plus I want you to meet them."

"What if they don't like me?" I asked, looking down at my hands as I wrung them together.

This time Knox did scoff. "You don't trust me, Annie?"

"N-no, of course I do." I stuttered.

Knox pulled to a stop, parking outside what I could only assume was his friends house. Knox unbuckled, turning to face me now as he spoke, "They're my friends. I'll make them be nice. You don't need to worry, just trust me." His tone held enough promise, all I could do was nod my head in response.

Stepping out of the car, I gazed up at the house before me. Everything about it could be classified as fairly standard. It was a two-story, suburban-like home that almost perfectly matched the rest of the quiet neighborhood. Nothing was out of place - even the leaves on the grass matched the pattern of the leaves on the lawn next door.

A gentle hand met the skin of my waist. I swallowed as Knox led me to the front door, not bothering to knock or ring the bell. Stepping over the threshold, I could hear muffled arguing that had to coming from the second floor.

Knox rolled his eyes at the sound, shouting "Liam" up the stairs before continuing to lead me through to the kitchen.

"Drink, Annie?" Knox asked, opening the fridge as I lingered by the edge of the counter a step away from him.

"Could I have chocolate milk, please?" I asked, not thinking about how childish of drink that was to request.

To my relief, Knox just grinned. "With those manners, how could I say no?" He teased.

I fought down my blush as he pulled out the milk and chocolate sauce. I stood at the counter in front of it, waiting as Knox grabbed a cup a spoon from the cabinets. Caging me from behind, Knox began mixing everything before me.

I wanted to protest - argue that I could've made it for myself - but the gentle caress of a light kiss meeting to tip of my ear had the words dying on my tongue.

"My good girl." Knox whispered as he plopped the chocolate milk into my hands.

My stomach clenched and breath hitched at his words. Heat crawled up my neck as I quickly tried to drown myself in my cup of milk. I couldn't bare looking in Knox's direction as he put everything away and my heart was still racing a couple minutes later when I set the empty cup down.

I was thankfully saved from having to speak as the sound of footsteps roared down the stairs. Before I could even blink, a tall dirty-blonde haired boy was panting as he leaned against the door frame of the kitchen.

"Get this fucker away from me." He ground out, looking at Knox. "He won't accept that I beat him at a fucking game and now he's trying to fight me."

An even louder set of footsteps sounded behind him as a slightly taller, dark-haired boy appeared behind him. "Liam shut the fuck up. You cheated like a pathetic little bitch and you know it."

"At least I don't whine like a bitch." Newly declared Liam mocked back.

"Watch your bastard mouth before I put a fist through your face." The taller one threatened, his face darkening with his words.

I took a hesitant step back, my eyes darting back and forth between the two. If these were Knox's friends, I certainly felt underprepared to meet them.

My movement seemed to draw both of their attention as their arguing came to an abrupt halt, both of them snapping their mouths closed. I could have cried then and there as both of them raked their eyes over me. Utter confusion contorting their features.

"Stop fucking looking at her." Knox ground out.

Liam continued to stare me down as the dark-haired one turned to face Knox once again. A wicked amusement filled his face, nearing an almost grin.

"We don't come to school for a few days and you get yourself a cute little girlfriend." He teased, smirking.

Liam snapped his head to look at Knox now, also grinning.

"She looks too sweet for you Knox-y boy. Where'd you find her?" Liam laughed, eyes sliding back to me.

"Shut the fuck up, Liam. Don't act like you're not wrapped around Clarissa's pinkie like a stupid little bitch." Knox spat, taking a threatening step in his direction.

Liam only laughed again, taking a step back with his hands in the air.

The other boy only rolled his eyes, a smirk still playing on his lips as he turned around to enter another room I couldn't see. Liam followed a few steps behind him before Knox turned to me.

Knox held out his hand expectantly, his face a lot softer than just moments before as he said, "C'mere, Annie."

I merely shook my head. Wide-eyed and completely frozen in my spot, I had absolutely no desire to follow wherever those two had gone off to. It took all my strength to not burst out crying now where I stood, there was no way I could stand being around them much longer.

Knox approached me, stopping just a breath away.

"I'm scared." I admitted in a barely audible whisper.

"They won't hurt you." Knox promised, tucking a loose hair behind my ear. "Be my good girl and sit with me on the couch?" Knox asked, his voice matching the softness of my whisper.

I frowned, my body feeling heavy with stress.

"Please?" Knox's breath hitting my ear as he leaned in. The one extra ask had my barriers breaking as I nodded my head 'yes'.

Knox held my hand as he led me through to the living room where the two boys now sat, loading up another video game on the giant tv. There was an oversized couch-like chair in the corner than Knox pulled to sit on with him.

There wasn't much moving space with the two of us sitting together, leaving us pressed up against each other. Knox wrapped his arm around me, pulling me into his side which under normal circumstances would leave me almost shaking in fear but now only brought me comfort to the already overwhelmingly stressful situation I was in.

The other two boys sat lazily stretched out on the main couch, clearly having forgotten all about their previous argument.

Now in what seemed to be their natural habitat, they looked far less intimidating than moments before. They faces no longer held the mischief or malice and were instead replaced with pure concentration.

I chewed on my thumb nail out of nervous habit as my eyes roamed over them, studying.

The dark-haired one - who I still didn't know the name of - cursed at the tv as Liam grinned. "I told you I wasn't cheating, just admit you suck, Sean."

Sean flashed his teeth mockingly, tossing aside the controller. "I'm done playing this shit."

His attention then turned to me as he leaned forward, his elbows resting on his knees. "What's your name anyways?" He asked, pulling out a paper bag from his jacket pocket.

I swallowed thickly, opening my mouth to answer when Knox's voice cut me off, "None of your fucking business." His chest vibrating beneath me as he spoke.

Sean scoffed, nearly throwing his head back, "Geez, I can't even know her name?" He laughed unbelievingly as he shook his head.

"Annie." I forced out, my voice sounding just as strained as it felt.

Sean hummed as he pulled out a lighter and a brown stick from the bag. A strong scent tickled my nose, making me scrunch it in distaste.

"Annie." Sean spoke, over-enunciating every syllable as he tested my name out on his tongue. He dragged his eyes over to Knox, "No need to get so worked up, Knox, nobody's trying to steal her from you." He laughed, pulling brown stick up to his mouth and burning the other end.

"What is that?" I asked, my curiosity overpowering my feelings of stupidity.

This time Liam chuckled. "You want to try some?" He asked, his eyes now sparking with interest.

"Fuck off." Knox said with far less aggression than moments before.

"Can I not have it?" I asked, looking up at Knox with confusion.

"Don't worry about it, baby." He soothed quietly in my ear.

I was on the verge of arguing but the look Knox gave me told me the conversation was final. I looked at Sean again as smoke puffed out of his mouth, his eyes already growing red and hazy.

Swallowing thickly, I realized maybe Knox was right after all.

A/N

I hope you guys enjoyed the extra long part!! Let me know what you think so far, I'd love to hear it. I can't believe the next part is already chapter 10!! I love and appreciate y'all so much so and I'm so grateful for y'all sticking around and reading this far!! xoxo - KATT

10

K nox's pov

In all honesty, I wasn't really sure why I invited Annie with me to Liam's house. Besides just wanting her around, there wasn't any real reason I had her come along. If anything, I probably shouldn't have invited her. Although Liam and Sean are my friends, they're not exactly the kind of people I would expect Annie to want to spend time with.

When I texted her this morning, I hadn't really given it more than a split second thought.

Not that I regretted it. Having her cuddled into my side was something I was more than happy to experience, but the second Liam and Sean laid eyes on her, a deep possessiveness came washing over me.

Possessiveness was something I'd struggled with since I was a toddler. But, it never usually transcended the little things. I mean I'd had girlfriends in the past but none of them made me feel this primal desire to possess or control them.

In fact, I didn't like to think of myself as controlling at all. I prided myself on not giving a fuck. Maybe that's why none of my relationships lasted very long.

Annie, though, was making these vices rear their ugly heads right in my direction. And she wasn't even my girlfriend. Well, not technically. She was mine, though. Even if she didn't know it yet.

Regardless, I needed to not let this ache to possess her control me. Annie is a real person, a sweet girl, a kind soul. I may desire her with every fiber of my being but that didn't mean I could go about controlling her. No, I wouldn't direct her decisions by any means. Nor do I have any desire to restrict her life.

All I want is for her to be mine, to own her thoughts just as much as her body. And I couldn't really see what was so wrong with that.

Annie's pov

My leg bounced the entire ride to school like usual. Even if I was starting to make a bit of progress, especially in terms of making it through the school day, I wasn't sure if it was something I'd ever truly get used to. It certainly didn't feel any easier.

I tugged on the ends of my forrest green sweater, smoothed out my black skirt, and fiddled with my headband before repeating the entire process again. I couldn't get my self to stop moving, to sit still.

Visions of the day before continued to flash through my mind. Liam and Sean had been unexpected acquaintances and certainly weren't my favorite people, but I was grateful that Knox wanted to give me a glimpse into his world. Maybe his choice of friends should have had me rethinking how much I thought I knew Knox but people are allowed to be multidimensional. If he wants to have friends like them, that didn't mean he couldn't also have a friend like me.

Getting out of the car, I bid Serena a 'goodbye' before making my way up the front steps. My breath hitched as my eyes met Knox's. He sat on the bench, reclining lazily. Maybe it was vain of me to assume he was just waiting for my arrival, but I only felt validated as he started to stand up at me approaching.

"C'mere pretty girl." Knox said, holding out his hand to me.

I gladly accepted it, far more comfortable with the feel of his calloused hands against mine.

"Hi." I squeaked out, a bit dazed as I looked up at him.

I stayed silent by his side as Knox led me through the hallway, not yet busy with students as it was still too early for class. My eyes only widened as Liam and Sean came into view, bickering as they stood leaning against the locker Knox was directly headed for.

Knox released my hand, instead using it to input his locker combination and sift through his stuff. An underlying panic bubbled within me at the loss of contact. I tried gulping it down as I stepped closer to hook my finger through one of his belt loops.

"Annie, don't you look adorable." Liam whistled, his eyes running me up and down.

My skin blanched embarrassingly. I jumped in my skin slightly as Knox slammed his locker door shut, shooting daggers in Liam's direction.

"Stop talking to her before I punch your fucking face." Knox threatened calmly - as calmly as a threat like that could sound. I nearly gasped at his words, shocked he would speak so roughly to someone he considered a friend.

"It was just a compliment." Liam laughed, crossing his arms.

Knox scoffed, sliding his arm around my waist. The heat of his hand sending shivers down my spine. He flashed Liam a crude gesture, only making Liam laugher harder as Knox turned us around to walk me to class.

Each lesson remained just as uneventful as the last.

I was still not having the easiest time focusing but it seemed like people were starting to get used to me being by Knox's side now. The stares had lessened considerable since last week and for that I was eternally grateful. I wasn't sure how much longer I could've lasted if that continued to be my daily experience.

Once lunch arrived, we sat at the same table as before. Only this time, Liam and Sean joined us. Knox switched to share my side of the bench, sparing me from having to be too close to either of the other boys.

I felt stiff and unnatural in my own skin, hyper aware of the size and proximity of the boys across from me.

I drew a shuddered breath as I began to unpack my lunch. I tried my best to avoid looking at them, even if they didn't make that task easy. They were loud, crude, and their presence could be felt even in the air around them.

A low whistle rung through my ears.

Peaking up, I saw Sean shaking his head at a smirking Liam. He was staring across the field at a girl who turned around to wave.

"Lara is low, even for you, Liam." Sean said, rolling his eyes as he bit into the burger he got from the cafeteria.

Liam scoffed, "You're just jealous she wouldn't do you."

Sean swallowed his bite, rolling back his shoulders as a disgusted sneer took over his face. "I wouldn't touch her even if she was laid up in my bed with her legs spread. Which I'm sure she'd do willingly if I so much as blinked in her direction."

I nearly choked on my sandwich, my hand coming up to cover my mouth. Did they always talk this way about women? If so, I was already beginning to lose my appetite.

"She's better than Rebecca Kline." Liam reasoned, staring down at his tray as he picked at his fries.

"Yeah right. Good luck pulling her." Sean argued.

"You think I couldn't?" Liam shot him a challenging glare.

I shifted uncomfortably, glancing at Knox who was too busy scrolling his phone to be paying attention the conversation before us.

"Not a chance. Your shit face doesn't make up for the fact that you're a walking STD." Sean all but laughed out.

A subtle tug of a smile graced Knox's face - the only thing that hinted that he was paying the other two any mind. Liam, however, did not find anything Sean said to be amusing. Squaring off his shoulders, his mouth was set in a firm line.

"Fine, let's ask the only person here qualified to know if I have a shit face." Liam ground out bitterly as he turned his attention to me. "Annie, babe, do you think I have a shit face?" He asked.

I almost squeaked in fright as his eyes met mine, yet I couldn't bring myself to look away. My mouth opened and closed as I struggled to find my voice, very closely resembling a fish. I stuttered before clearing my throat, "I-I don't really know." I blinked, my eyes darting between Liam and Sean.

"Sure you do." Liam said, narrowing his eyes in seriousness.

I subtly inched closer to Knox, wringing my hands together. Liam's stare was becoming all too much and I was entirely too scared of saying the wrong thing. Isn't there such thing as intimidating the witness?

Sean's laugh spared me, "She just too much of a sweetheart to be mean to your jackass."

I gasped at the implication that I was calling Liam ugly, shaking my head. "I-I didn't say that."

Sean only laughed harder, clapping Liam on the back as he hunched over. Even Liam started to crack a smile.

"If you wanted to smoosh, Annie, you could've just said that." Liam chuckled, eyes glinting with amusement.

My face grew hot, no doubt burning bright red. Slowly I let out a small laugh, biting my tongue.

"Uh-oh, Annie, babe. I don't think Knox-y is too happy about our new found love. His big fat head can't comprehend how hot you find me." Liam mocked, nodding his head to a clearly unamused Knox.

I had to cover my mouth in an attempt to stifle my laugh. Heat bloomed in my chest as Knox looked down at me, his face instantly softening.

Gently snaking his arm around my waist, his hand softly squeezed my side as he leaned down to whisper, his warm breath tickling my ear, "When are you going to smile for me like that?" My stomach clenched as my skin blanched yet again.

The pure need, the pure desire mixed with the envy of my smile being for somebody else that dripped from his words had me nearly unraveling. I felt like putty in his hands - clay that only his hands could mould. The look he gave me in the moment told me there was truly no going back.

A/N

AHHH bonus extra chapter this week!!! I hope you guys liked a hint into Knox's pov. I know I kept that part short but I just wanted to give a brief glimpse into how he's thinking and maybeee I'll include another glimpse later on. Let me know what you think and once again I'm so grateful for all of you!! xoxox - KATT

11

Tuesday and Wednesday passed in a blur.

I managed two more successful days of attending all my classes. Classes were starting to pick up now, assigning more and more work. I still wouldn't say that any of this feels normal - certainly not how it used to a few months ago - but I was starting to get more used to it.

It was becoming my new normal and so far, I felt okay with that.

Even Sean and Liam are starting to grow on me. I was just now starting to understand that their bickering is more playful than anything serious. Their words remain harsher than any I would use and they bicker far more than I would've expected from people who call each other friends, but they didn't seem as bad as I first thought.

Knox was my quiet calm, effectively balancing out every anxiety I felt on a daily basis.

His soft touches, lingering stare, and gentle words only further fueled my growing appreciation for him. I was becoming so used to his presence that my chest started aching with emptiness when he was no longer around.

"You're more quiet than usual today." Serena said, pulling out of my day dream.

My forehead laid against the cool glass of the car window as my eyes came back in to focus, looking at the quickly passing buildings. My eyes now burning, I blinked rapidly as I pulled my head away.

"I'm just tired." I replied, rubbing one of my eyes with the back of my hand.

It was the truth. Attending school was absorbing almost all of my available energy and using up every ounce of my focus.

"You haven't mentioned anything about school - about how you're feeling." Serena's voice shook slightly with hesitation.

"I'm doing my best." I frowned.

"I know - I don't mean that. I just mean, I want to make sure you're feeling okay. I don't want to push you too hard." Serena's eyes shifted between me and the road a few times.

"It's exhausting but I'm getting through." I said, mustering up the best smile I could.

In all honesty, I wasn't quite sure how I was feeling. As much as I was starting to get used to the situation I was forced to be in, I couldn't figure out what I actually thought about it on a deeper level. For the most part - besides my newfound friend - I didn't really enjoy going to school and if I was given the choice, I still would prefer to finish my degree online.

I mean I am a bit proud of myself for getting through and being able to handle it so far but I didn't think I was doing a particularly great job. I still feel constantly on edge and overwhelmingly anxious at almost every moment of the school day. If this is how it was going to be for the rest of the school year, I couldn't say that I was really looking forward to it.

The answer to this question felt so complex, I was still thinking about it as I sat down on the brown leather couch of Wendy's office.

"Annie." Wendy beamed in greeting as she too took her seat across from me.

I tilted my head slightly, lips thinning as I stared back silently. I could tell my lack of greeting bothered her but I could find it in myself to care too much.

Wendy's eye twitched slightly before she spoke again, "So, it's been a week since you started school..." she prompted, "tell me how that's going."

I eyed the pen that gleamed in her right hand. I swallowed thickly and shifted slightly in my seat but still couldn't find an answer in me that was worth speaking.

"Annie," Wendy sighed greatly, "I know you aren't too happy with me since I suggested that you go back to attending in person, but I hope you can understand that I am here to help you. I have your best interests at heart." She urged, the smile now gone from her face.

I grimaced. Help. My knuckles fisted on my lap. I had to literally bite my tongue to stop myself from saying how badly I did not want her help. My silence felt even louder than before as she continued to stare at me without blinking.

"Have you at least made any friends?" Wendy asked. Her voice was becoming increasingly more firm. I was irritating her and she wasn't bothering to hide it anymore.

Knox's face flashed through my mind. My insides instantly felt warmer. Sighing, I gave in.

"One." I finally said.

Wendy's eyes flashed with surprise, her pen hanging loosely - forgotten between our one-sided squabble and her new revelation.

"And... how did you meet her?"

I glanced out the window to my left, her eye contact becoming too intense. I thought about not correcting her - thought about letting her go on believing that the friend I made was a girl - but for once I found myself wanting to show her my progress.

"H-he - uh - he's been helping me get around school." I admitted quietly, refocusing my attention on Wendy just in time to see shock light up her face. I could tell she tried to hide it a second later but she didn't do a very good job.

"His name is Knox." I offered up, hoping that talking about him more would fix the awkwardness that now filled the air around us.

"And Knox is your friend?" Wendy asked. She was trying to recover herself as quickly as she could but she still sounded dumbfounded as she spoke. Confusion and utter disbelief seeping through her every word.

I nodded my head. "He's very nice..." I hesitated as I thought back to his interactions with Liam and Sean. "Well, nice to me." I altered.

"And how is he nice to you?" She asked not looking up. Remembering her pen, she started scribbling quickly on her note pad.

"H-He looks out for me in the hallways..." I started, looking away again briefly as I thought back. "He got my schedule changed so he could help bring me to my classes...He knows I don't like being around boys." I responded quietly.

"You told him about your fear?" Wendy questioned further, continuing to write passionately.

"Well," I hesitated, "I think he just picked up on it. He said he'd punch his friend because he was speaking to me." Even as the words left my mouth, I knew I was going to regret them.

Wendy's brows shot straight up, I would've laughed if it were a cartoon - or if it wasn't a reaction to something I had just said.

"He sounds violent, Annie." She gasped out.

I stuttered, trying to recover. "He's really not! I-I didn't explain it well." I furrowed my brows worriedly as I struggled to find the words to explain. Knox wasn't violent - or at least he wasn't a threat to me. He'd only threatened to punch Liam because it was clear that I was uncomfortable. He wouldn't have done that for any other reason. He had to have just picked up on my fear and was defending me.

"You're okay with him speaking like this?" Wendy asked incredulously.

"He's not violent. He wouldn't hit me." I ground out, growing more frustrated with not only Wendy but also myself. This is exactly why I don't share anything with her. She's making this into something that it's not.

"Annie," She massaged her temple as she spoke, "I know you don't like talking about your abandonment issues but you have to be more aware of who you let yourself get attached to. If you've only known this boy for a few days and he's already threatened to hit someone, you need to step back from him. He sounds like a bad influence and I don't want to see you getting wrapped up in it." She urged.

"Knox is my friend and he treats me well." I said curtly as I crossed my arms and leaned back into the couch. "I'm done talking."

Knox was the only one who bothered looking out for me throughout the school day. The only one who went out of his way to make sure that I felt safe and comfortable. The only one. There would be absolutely no way that Wendy could convince me that Knox was a bad influence.

Knox is my friend. Mine. And I'm not going to let her take him away from me.

He's already helping me get better. Wendy should be praising me for going out of my comfort zone - should be praising me for working to be better like she claims she wants me to be.

But she's not and for that reason, consider this session over.

12

Wendy's words imbedded themselves in my mind just like I knew she wanted them to. Only instead of making me rethink my friendship with Knox, her words only made me ache to be around him that much more.

All throughout the next school day I felt an even greater pull to be around Knox than normal.

I found my eyes lingering longer every time I glanced his way. I unconsciously scooted my desk chair closer to him in every class. And every time we walked through the hallways, I reached for his hand instead of the seam of his shirt.

Knox didn't seem to mind, though. At least not from what I could tell. I suppose if my extra clinginess was bothering him, he could have shaken me off at any point.

Even at lunch time I sat with only a breath between us. The hair on my arms standing up with acute awareness of our close proximity.

Pulling out my ham sandwich, I let my eyes take in Knox's appearance for the hundredth time today. He wore a black graphic tee that showed off just the bottom of the tattoo I had yet to fully see. The swirls of black ink twirling up his bicep and out of sight peaked my curiosity.

Trailing my eyes up to his face, I tilted my head slightly at the focused look on his face. He was staring intently at something on his phone, his gaze unmoving.

My eyes narrowed and I couldn't help the frown that started to grow. Irritation bubbled at the back of my throat. I wanted his attention, I just didn't know how to get it. Shifting where I sat, I let out a small puff of frustration before taking another bite of my sandwich.

In an instant Knox wound an arm around my waist, drawing me flush against his side. I instinctively loosed a small squeak of surprise at the contact.

"What's got my girl in such a huffy puffy mood, hm?" He asked, not breaking his gaze from his phone screen. His was voice teasing and low so only I could hear him. Not that it mattered as Liam and Sean had long since left to get their lunch from the cafeteria.

I forced myself to swallow my bite. My eyes were wide as I gazed up at his face without answering. My silence had his head turning to look at me. His eyes glinted darkly as he took me in. My heart was beating rapidly - so hard I thought it would burst from me at any second.

His fingers flexed as they dug softly into my side. His palm effectively warming my skin beneath. I began to flush under his stare, squirming slightly in his hold.

Knox leaned down, his teeth nipping at my ear as he pulled me in closer. "Such at brat." He whispered, his breath tickling my neck as he spoke. "Tell me what's got my pouty girl in such a bad mood so I can fix it."

I gulped, my face and body now burning. A shudder escaped me as he pressed a ghost of a kiss beneath my ear. I licked my lips, almost throwing myself back against him as he started to pull away. Playfully pinching my side, his expectant look prompted me to speak.

"I-I-" I stuttered, struggling to come up with a less embarrassing explanation for my attitude. Even if I mainly just wanted his sole attention back on me, it would be too mortifying to say just that.

His thumb started to draw soft, lazy circles on my hip - only muddling my mind further. The smile that tugged at his lips told me that he knew exactly what he was doing.

"Y-you're not eating anything." I offered up pathetically.

"I'm not hungry." The corner of his lip twitched, amusement growing in his eyes.

"Bu-but you can't not eat." I all but whined, sounding increasingly pathetic to even my own ears.

"What're you suggesting I have?" He asked lowly, an almost predatory look flashing across his face. The nature of his suggestion going right over my head as I reached for the untouched half of my sandwich and pushed it over in front of him.

"I'm not eating your lunch, Annie." Knox frowned.

"Why not? It's really good, I promise." I pouted slightly.

"It's for you, not me." He furrowed his brows about to push it back to me before my hand met his to stop the movement.

"Please..." I practically begged, jutting out my bottom lip as I pouted.

"Fine." He grumbled before taking a bite.

I beamed, happy to have not only won but also to have gotten out of my original predicament successfully. I finished off my half of the sandwich, looking around the field with mild interest before Knox's voice met my ears again.

"Brat." He teasingly grumbled under his breath, causing me to snap my head to look at him once again.

My mouth opened and closed, gaping at his accusation.

"No?" He asked, leaning back down to whisper in my ear. "My girl's not a whiny little brat who pouts until she gets her way?" He lightly bit down on my ear, a small strangled noise effectively escaping from the back of my throat.

I nearly whined as he pulled away. My body now feeling heavy as I was moulded into his side.

I felt sluggish and unable to focus the rest of the school day. My stomach was in knots that only tightened further every time Knox looked at me. I could hardly hold a pencil with the way my body felt so weak under his stare.

"Let me drive you home." He said as we reached the bottom of the stairs in front of the school.

I could only nod my head sleepily before he led me to his car. I was barely sat down for all of 30 seconds before my body started to sag against the car door and I nodded off.

The feeling of the car coming to a park had me all but jerking awake.

I was rubbing the sleep from my eyes with the back of my hand when the feeling of Knox's finger tips brushing my hair behind my ear tickled my skin. I loosed a sigh as I unconsciously leaned into the touch.

"I'll see you tomorrow, Annie." He said, his voice just above a whisper.

I hummed, not completely content. Even if it was a promise - one I could believe - I still didn't want him to go. His presence made me feel so warm and I wasn't ready for that feeling to stop just yet.

"Do you want to come inside?" I asked without thinking my question through completely. I'd been alone with Knox before but this was different. This was my home - my safe space. Inviting a boy in should have felt wrong but somehow it didn't.

Knox followed me up the stairs to my room. The house was silent save for the creaking floorboards under our feet. Serena was still at work and would be for a couple more hours. I probably should have let her know that I was inviting my friend in with me but even now the thought failed to cross my mind.

My whole body felt stiff - unnatural. It wasn't a testament to Knox in the slightest. I still had the same warm, safe feeling as I always did with him but the idea having any boy, even Knox, in my room was terrifying.

I stepped aside to let Knox walk in first, let him take in my room by himself.

I hesitated, lingering at the door. Often I left it closed when I was in my room but even now, when I knew I could trust Knox more than any other boy, I couldn't bring myself to shut it. Just the idea of shutting myself off in here with just him had my lungs swelling uncomfortably and my palms sweating uncontrollably.

Standing in the middle of my room, Know turned around to look at me. The softness of his face and the hint of a smile tugging at the corner of his mouth was just the little encouragement I needed to step out of the door way and into my room.

I set my backpack down next to my desk as Knox's eyes danced around my room. Walking to my bookshelf, he let his fingers brush against the spines of my books and stopped just as one caught his attention.

My fingers twitched when he pulled it out and looked at the cover of my diary.

Wendy had recommended I start one after everything first happened. Since I wasn't as forthcoming in talking to her, she wanted me to at least process my thoughts somehow. So I did it for weeks, arguably the most dark weeks of my life. Even all these months later, the thought of rereading those thoughts had me unnerved which is why I never planned to pick it up again.

I could see Knox hesitate as he stared at the cover. My heart raced, my mind whirling as I wanted nothing more in this moment than to know what he was thinking as he stared at it.

And then he put it back.

I forced myself to swallow, my mouth turning completely dry. I push down the part of me that wanted him the ask to read it - the part of me that wanted him to want to understand me.

"Cute." Knox said, startling me. He flashed me a teasing grin as he gestured to the teddy bear that laid on my pillows. I blanched, turning away.

"I'm nervous." I blurted. The words that had been lodged uncomfortably in my throat since we stepped into the house, now loose and turned into word vomit.

Knox furrowed his brows, his face turning serious.

"Because of me?" He asked.

I gulped, nodding my head slightly. Several moments of silence slipped between us as he surveyed me.

"Do you want me to go?" His body twitched in the direction of the door.

"No." I almost gasped, putting my hands up as if to stop him. "No, I just - I just am not used to..." I trailed off, not sure how to describe our situation.

Knox seemed to understand as he took in my words.

"What do you normally do when you get nervous like this?"

I twisted my hands in front of myself, thinking.

"I paint." I admitted.

"Then, let's paint."

13

Every few seconds, I found myself glancing at Knox nervously as I sat down on my carpeted floor. Pulling out the paint, brushes, and canvases I have stored under my bed, I laid them out in front of me.

"You don't have anything to put down to protect the carpet?" Knox asked as he sat down across from me.

I eyed the arms length of distance between us, my heart still beating furiously. I passed him a canvas and small paint pallet before placing my set of brushes between us to share.

"It's okay if it gets messy." I shrugged, missing the way Knox's eyebrows shot up in mild surprise.

Carefully, I unboxed my paints and mindfully started selecting my palate.

I started to get so absorbed in the ideas floating around my head, I almost completely forgot that Knox was even there. With a pencil in hand, I drew out a sketch of a vase of my favorite flowers, Lilies. It's not something I would usually paint but I found comfort in the simplicity of the idea.

I was just about to grab a brush when Knox's voice startled me as it reached my ears. "How often do you paint?" He asked.

I spared him a glance, he was seemingly just as equally invested in his canvas. He had already adorned his pallet with paints and he didn't so much as look up as he asked the question.

"Not as much as I used to but sometimes." I said, trying and failing to peak at what he had started to paint on his canvas. He had it angled just enough away from me so I couldn't see what it was.

I refocused my attention on my lilies. I took my time, letting myself get lost in each stoke. I wasn't particularly skilled at painting but I did find solace in creating something that didn't always have to be perfect. This was a different kind of therapy for me - one that didn't make me feel quite so broken inside.

Soon enough I found my heart rate evening out and my nerves settling - almost comfortable.

It didn't last long, however, as I flicked my brush just a bit too hard and some of the paint flew threw the air and splattered on Knox's arm. I gasped, my eyes growing wide.

Knox looked down at the giant green blob on his otherwise clean arm before meeting my horrified gaze. I opened my mouth to apologize but before I could, he flicked his own brush in my direction. A giant glob of yellow paint hurled at me.

I jerked back in shock, gaping between Knox and the paint that now sat on my leg. Any form of apology I was planning to say abruptly died on my tongue.

"Knox!" I gasped, "Mine was an accident!" I looked down at the mess, gaping like a fish - unsure what exactly to do.

"Mine was too. Just like this one." Knox mocked.

I looked up just in time to watch him flick more paint at me, splattering all down my arm.

I sputtered in astonishment. Gritting my teeth at his audacity, I scooped up a giant bit of paint and lunged at his face. He raised his hands, clearly taken by surprise, but I successfully landed a thick line down his cheek.

Knox bit his tongue, a new fire dancing in his eyes as he dipped his fingers into his pallet. Having completely abandoned his brush, he smeared paint all down both my arms with his bare hands.

My breath hitched as the coldness of the paint coated me. Knox barking out a laugh after he pulled away.

It became a completely frenzy after that. Each of us took handfuls of paint and smeared them on whatever part of each other we could reach. From his arms, to my cheek, to his neck, it continued to go back and forth until we were almost completely covered.

I made one last move to rub my paint-covered hands through his hair before I attempted to get up and make a run for it. I hadn't even stood up yet before Knox was on me with his own paint-covered hands pulling me into him.

I felt a familiar panic tingle through my body as I frantically tried to escape his grasp. Gasping for breath, I feebly pushed at his chest. Knox didn't notice, though. His laughter still filled the room as he pulled me into his lap, holding me around the waist and the back of my neck.

My eyes stung with tears that had already begun trailing down my cheeks. The laughter stopped abruptly as we finally came face-to-face.

My hands fisted his shirt as my breathing shallowed - each breath requiring more effort than the last. Ringing filled my ears and my brain turned fuzzy.

I could feel tears grow heavier as they trailed down my face, taking some of the paint with them.

"Annie?" Knox's worried voice sounded muffled and barely audible compared to the incessant ringing. His hands moved to hold my face, concern overtaking his features. Sobs wracked my body as he held me, rocking slightly.

My knuckles turned white from gripping his shirt so tightly. My eyes were completely blurry and my body burned as he held me. I knew something like this was possible to happen from the moment we stepped into the house but I had so much hope it wouldn't. I thought with Knox it might turn out differently and even now I felt confused - my body felt confused.

For as much as I was panicking because of Knox, he also was the only thing calming me down.

We stayed there sitting on the floor, rocking together, until my tears started to slow and my breathing eventually evened out into sporadic, breathy hiccups.

Everything now felt numb and heavy as he held me. My body buzzed like tv static while my mind lulled blankly. He stroked my hair gently, cooing in my ear until I felt almost relaxed.

Eventually, he stood up. Still holding me, he walked into my bathroom and set me on the counter. I didn't dare a glance in the mirror - so sure that I looked hysterical. Neither of us said anything as Knox grabbed a washcloth and wet it under the sink before beginning to work at getting the paint off my skin.

I almost couldn't bare looking him in the eyes but once I did, the emotions they held startled me. I expected him to be feeling a lot of different ways after what just happened but the last thing I expected was him to be so full of guilt. His brows were drawn tensely as he washed the paint off me which only amplified the sadness that rimmed his irises.

"I'm sorry." I whispered hoarsely. My voice sounding strained after all my crying.

The guilt of him being witness to my breakdown was only growing. I thought I could have a boy, at least Knox, in my house without having a whole panic attack - thought I had moved pasted this at least a little bit.

Knox didn't say anything, his frown only deepening.

He didn't look at me again as he now started cleaning himself, mainly focusing on the larger chucks. Setting the cloth aside a few minutes later, some smaller bits still clung to his skin.

He sighed as he stepped between my legs, hands going on either side of me as if he was now afraid to touch me. I looked at him through my still-wet lashes, biting my lip as I waited for him to say something - anything.

"C'mon, Annie. You should sleep." He said softly, barely glancing up at me for a second before looking away again.

I opened my mouth, wanting nothing more than to argue - to have him stay here and talk through this with me so I could explain everything. I wanted to make him know that it wasn't his fault. I wanted to say anything that would take away the guilt that lingered in his eyes.

But he didn't give me the chance as he stepped away from me, holding out a hand to help me off of the counter. My legs wobbled as I stood. My blood rushed to my head, the makings of a headache now pounding against my skull.

Maybe now really wasn't the time to talk yet.

Knox helped me into my bed, making sure I was tucked in. I knew it wouldn't be right of me to ask him to stay - not after what just happened - but I almost couldn't help myself.

I barely started to open my mouth but he was quick to cut me off before I could get a word out.

"I'll pick you up tomorrow afternoon, okay?" He said, brushing his knuckles against my cheek.

I nodded my head, biting my tongue. Tomorrow is fine. Talking tomorrow was infinitely better than never talking again. I could deal with tomorrow.

Knox send me the smallest, sweetest smile that melted me just enough to have me snuggle further into my bed and drift right off to sleep.

14

Serena was exceptionally worried when she got home and saw me sleeping. The dark eye bags and red-rimmed eyes didn't help my case either.

As soon as I woke up, she went on a long monologue about how maybe she was putting too much pressure on me all at once. I didn't bother to correct her - didn't bother to explain why I had actually been so worn out in the first place. It would take too much explaining that I couldn't stomach yet.

I felt bad about not filling her in but not bad enough to actually do it. I would tell her eventually, just not when it was still so fresh.

I still felt extremely guilty for how everything went down with Knox. The fact that I invited him into the house and then freaked out on him was humiliating. He deserves an explanation and I was aching to give it to him.

But for now I'd just have to wait with the promise that I'd see him tomorrow.

That night Serena made me my favorite spaghetti dinner and we stayed up well into the evening watching our favorite trashy reality tv shows. If anything, I was immensely grateful for the way that Serena knew how to get my mind off of things. Even when she didn't fully know what was going on, she always knew how to fix it and leave a smile on my face.

The next morning was a difficult one. I had slept well only in the sense that I had been so emotionally exhausted, I passed out immediately. As for everything else, nightmares plagued me the whole night to point where I felt almost more tired when I woke up than when I had first gone to sleep.

Serena started to invite me to run errands with her, but upon seeing my state suggested I take the morning to relax after all.

So, I did just that.

I took a long bubble bath, lit a candle, and played soft music as I tried to take my mind off the impending conversation with Knox. It had worked to an extent. My body felt thoroughly relaxed and there was thankfully no trace of paint from the day before.

My mind, however, could not shake the trickles of anxiety that seeped their way in.

I was standing outside on the curb a couple hours later, waiting for Knox to pick me up like he had texted earlier. I fiddled with the sleeve of my cream sweater before brushing down the skirt of my white dress for the millionth time since I put it on. I straightened my necklace and pushed back my hair, shifting my weight as I spotted his car approaching.

As he pulled up the curb in front of me, I took a steadying deep breath before opening the car door. The air from his a/c hit my warm cheeks, already beginning to cool me down.

I felt bad when I avoided Knox's eye but I couldn't bare looking at his quite yet. Instead I zeroed in on my usually empty seat. My mouth parted slightly and my head tilted to the side in confusion. I glanced between the seat and Knox a couple times, trying and failing to process what this was about.

I noticed Knox suppressing a smile as he reached across the center console and picked up the bouquet of flowers so that I could sit down.

Swallowing thickly, I tried not to think about who they were for as I buckled myself in. Knox handed them back to me once I was situated - obviously not able to hold them and drive simultaneously. I bit my lip as I stared at the arrangement full of soft pink and white flowers.

An overwhelming sense of bitterness filled my body the longer I admired them.

"Whoever these are for must be lucky." The words left my mouth before I could stop them. I cringed internally as my voice sounded bitter even to my own ears.

To my absolute horror, Knox burst out laughing. His whole face contorted in amusement. The sight was one of the most beautiful things I'd ever seen - it almost successful distracted me from my jealousy. Almost but not quite.

"Annie, baby, I got them for you." He laughed softly, shaking his head as if he could believe I would have thought otherwise.

"Oh," I said dumbly, furrowing my brows in confusion and embarrassment. I looked down at the flowers again and what was once bitterness now blossomed into warmth that spread throughout my entire body.

"Oh." I said again, now understanding why he had placed them on the seat for me. "Thank you." I whispered, mortification seeping into my veins.

Knox smiled but didn't take his eyes off the road. He cleared his throat, his tone growing more serious, "I'm sorry about yesterday. I shouldn't have been so rough and crossed so many boundaries. It was wrong of me."

I blinked as I stared at the side of his face. I failed to come up with a response as I took in his apology. No boy I had ever met had ever apologized for something like that - never would any of them have even dreamed to do that.

My bottom lip wobbled at the realization, his words still echoing in my mind.

Knox pulled into the same park we had gone to the week before and parked in the same spot. He turned to look at me before gently wiping away a stray tear from my face with his thumb.

"I was assaulted a few months ago." I whispered. My voice came out wobbly and shook with the pain I still continued to feel from it, but I wanted him to understand now. I wanted him to know that his apology meant more to me than he could have ever known it would.

His body stilled at my admission, his hand leaving my face as he waited for me to continue.

"I still don't even really know what happened - my mind blocked out most of the details. I remember enough, though." I gulped, trying to fight the strain that threatened my voice. "He was like a brother to me, we were so close. I trusted him with every ounce of my being and he - he betrayed that trust."

"I'm sorry." Knox whispered as my eyes filled with tears again.

"I-I'm still scared all the time. People - boys - scare me. I don't like being touched. I don't like when people get too close to me. I feel on edge constantly. I-it's something I'm working on and maybe I won't be like this forever but it's still so hard." I continued, my voice now coming out more strained as I tried to fight off the sobs that threatened to take over.

"But I don't feel so bad when I'm with you..." I chanced a glance at Knox before looking down at my hands again, "You don't scare me so bad. I feel warm - safe - when I'm with you."

My confession hung in the air as I wiped away the tears that slid down my face. I felt pathetic for how often I cried in front of Knox, but I would be forever grateful that he didn't make me feel bad for it.

"If I ever make you uncomfortable, just say the word and I will stop whatever I'm doing no questions asked. And if there's someone else that's treating you any type of way that makes you scared, just say my name and I'll be there." Knox said, his tone firm and unyielding.

I nodded, letting out a small breath of relief.

"And if you can't speak, you hit that fucker as hard as you can - even me. Slap me in the face and I'll know why - I won't ever get mad." He promised.

I forced another nod before setting the flowers on the dash and crawling across the console. My eyes were completely blurred with tears so my actions were sloppy as I moved to sit in his lap. Now with me straddling him, Knox wrapped his arms around me and tucked my head against his chest.

I tried choking down my sobs but failed miserably. Knox rubbed my back and whispered soothing words as he held me nonetheless.

Maybe it was just my heightened emotions or my need to express gratitude or maybe I just wasn't thinking at all, but next thing I knew, I had pulled away from his chest and kissed his cheek.

Knox loosed a breath, eyes glinting as he took hold of my jaw and started littering kisses all over my face. He kissed all my remaining tears away before kissing my temple, my nose, and the corner of my mouth.

I squeaked, staring at him with wide-eyes at the final kiss.

He pulled away, eyes roaming my face as his thumb tugged at my bottom lip. I nearly whimpered before he leaned down and covered my lips with his own.

It wasn't my first kiss but I certainly had never had one like this before. It held so much passion and longing, I easily found myself getting lost in it.

And if this is what being lost is like, I never want to be found.

15

- -

The feeling of Knox's lips still lingered on mine the next day.

It's all I could think about as I tried going to sleep last night. I rolled around, kicking restlessly at my bed sheets for hours. Eventually I must have succumbed to sleep as I was now blinking awake.

As the morning glow filled my room and bounced off the flowers that sat so pristinely on my desk, the feeling of his kiss was back again.

I blanched even as there was no witness to my thought. Just the feeling alone causing my internal embarrassment. I let myself wonder if Knox could be having the same feeling - could be thinking about the feel of my lips on his as if they were still there and never really left.

This feeling carried me through the entire week. Not even my session with Wendy was able to bring down the sense of euphoria I carried with me.

She pried and pried to get me to talk and I relented slightly, but nothing about Knox - nothing about what I knew she really wanted to know. She still seemed skeptical of Knox and I didn't want to hear anything about it so I rightfully kept it all to myself.

It even happened again and again and even again. At random times throughout the day Knox would lean down to kiss me in one way or another. Sometimes on my temple or my cheek, sometimes on the corner of my mouth, and sometimes even giving me a full kiss as he had done in the car before.

I tried not to look too overcome with giddiness every time one of these moments happened but it was hard to contain. My crush on Knox was in full effect and was becoming hard to hide.

Not that it seemed that I needed to hide it anyway. I mean after all, it was Knox who was kissing me first - I just welcomed it with open arms.

Liam and Sean didn't seem to be the slightest bit surprised. They found it amusing, if not also totally disgusting. Their ceaseless teasing - mainly just Liam's - was unwavering and thankfully, mostly aimed at Knox.

If Liam had teased me nearly as much as he teased Knox, I would've been too embarrassed to ever show my face again.

We were even starting to fall into a routine now.

Everyday after school, Knox would either drive me home or bring me with him to Liam or Sean's house. There they would all play video games or put on car races and I would stay cuddled into Knox's side.

Serena was starting to get gradually more inquisitive. She knew I wasn't coming home right away every day and she also knew that I had gained some friends. Claiming that she noticed how exceptionally happy I had become more recently.

I thought about telling her and even came close to it a few times before I stopped myself. I wasn't trying to hold back for any particular reason, I just wasn't really sure what to refer to Knox as anymore. It seemed a bit wrong to just call him my friend as we had now established that we did in fact like to kiss each other, but he also wasn't quite my boyfriend. It just felt a bit easier to avoid the subject of our status altogether.

The Saturday a week after our first kiss, I woke up with a jolt at the sound of my phone ringing.

"Hello?" I mumbled, still groggy and half asleep. I didn't need to check the caller ID to know who it was.

"Baby..." Knox's voice purred through the phone, effectively making my stomach clench.

"Hi..." I whispered back without thinking, forgetting I had already said 'hello.'

His soft chuckle met my ears, "I'm pulling up to your house right now, be my good girl and let me in?"

I gasped, shooting straight up to look at the clock on my nightstand. It was already noon. I couldn't believe I had slept in so late. And Knox was coming over - in fact, was practically already there.

I left my phone forgotten on my bed as I dashed to the bathroom to brush my teeth and hair, and wash my face in record time. I barely put deodorant on when I heard his truck park outside. I bolted down the stairs, glancing around to find the house void of Serena and a note left on the counter.

Got pulled into a meeting today, will be back around dinner time :)

I let out a short breath of relief before a knock at the door sounded through the house. I didn't bother rushing to the door, not wanting to seem too eager in answering even if that was exactly what I had been doing the whole time.

Taking one more steadying breath, I smoothed down my hair once last time before I wrenched the door open to find Knox standing there in all his glory.

"Hi." I breathed out - no doubt sounding as dumb as I felt.

"Hi, Annie." He said, his breath coming out in half a laugh. His eyes raked over me, taking me in, as I stepped to the side to let him over the threshold. I squirmed where I stood, suddenly regretting not making the time to change before I came down stairs.

I led him up to my room, Knox trailing a pace behind me. I was a step away from reaching my dresser so I could pick clothes to change into when his hands met my waist and effectively stopped me.

Pulling me in against his chest, his warms hands roamed the sliver of bare skin between my tank top and shorts, sliding the top up slowly as he splayed his hand across my stomach. Hugging me from behind, he brushed his lips against my bare shoulder in a soft kiss before letting me go completely.

"My pretty girl." He hummed to himself as he sat down on my bed, his eyes still glued to me.

I all but stumbled to my dresser, body on fire as a blush burned my face. I pulled out the first thing I saw and was about to make my way to bathroom before Knox's hands caught my waist again. He pulled me to stand between his legs and I had to bring my arms to his shoulders to steady myself from the abrupt movement - the clothes in my hand dropping, forgotten, to his side.

His eyes grew dark, hungry, as they studied me. I found myself nearly squirming under his gaze yet again but did my best to hold it back. I bit my lip to hold back the noise I felt in the back of my throat as his hands slid up the side of my thighs and over my hips, his finger tips tickling my skin as they grazed by.

"Fuckin' hell, Annie." Knox all but groaned, his Adam's apple bobbing up and down as he swallowed. He let his head fall against my still bare stomach as his thumbs brushed the underside of my breasts, his breath tickling my belly. My own breath hitched at the touch but I felt no desire to pull away.

I hesitantly stroked my hand through his hair, letting my nails graze his scalp, before he lifted his head up again to look at me.

"Liam invited us over to swim at his house if you wanted to do that." Knox said, his voice straining as he forced the change of topic.

"Okay." I nodded half heartedly, still consumed with his lingering touch.

"Am I making you uncomfortable?" He asked a beat later, his hands growing still against my skin.

"No." I shook my head vigorously - probably too eagerly. Whatever he was doing, I didn't want him to stop now.

But he did anyways.

"Good. Go get changed." Loosing a breath, he gave my waist one last squeeze before dropping his hands and reaching for his phone.

I stood unmoving for a second too long as a small smirk started forming at the corner of his mouth. I frowned, embarrassment flooding my system. Willing myself to move, I went back to my dresser to grab a bikini before stalking off to bathroom to finally change.

16

K nox's fingers drummed against his steering wheel as he drove us to Liam's house. I fiddled with the end of my shorts, my legs tightly crossed as I sat in the passenger seat. A dull ache still lingered in the pit of my stomach from the feel of his hands - I tried to ignore it but was failing miserably.

I had grown familiar with Liam's house now as it was often the place we went the most after school. His parents had a habit of not being home and it was a spot well suited for entertaining.

Knox and I walked in but found the inside of the house to be empty. Knox made a move to grab my hand as he led us through the house but I strategically moved my hand out of his reach. Maybe it was petty - bratty, he liked to say - to throw a fit like this but I couldn't help unleashing the frustration he built up in me before we left.

His eyes narrowed as he clocked the movement but he didn't say anything. Instead he opened the sliding glass door, revealing Liam and Sean sitting on bar stools at an outdoor kitchenette.

I spotted another girl laid on a beach lounger in the sun, seemingly napping.

"Well if it isn't my favorite person." Sean grinned my way. I tried to hide my surprise as it was normally Liam who did the teasing. It was a rare occasion to see Sean in such a good mood - certainly a mood that would make him declare me his 'favorite person.'

I could practically hear Knox's eyes roll next to me.

"Hi, Sean." I greeted, smiling back at him.

If working Knox up was the only way I could get back at him for leaving me hanging like that then so be it. A dangerous game but one I was also willing to play.

Sean quirked a brow in mild surprise but his grin didn't falter. Knox ignored us as he walked around to a mini fridge hidden in the counter and grabbed a beer.

"Anything to drink, Annie?" Liam asked, being ever the most excellent host.

I shook my head, smiling 'thanks' in his direction. I could feel Knox's stare burning through the side of my head. How he could get worked up so easily when all I did was smile - at his friends no less - was beyond me.

Regardless, I was hoping to use it to my advantage.

Choosing to ignore him, I walked over to where the unknown girl laid. Setting the towel I brought down on the lounger next to hers, I confirmed that she was indeed napping. She was beautiful - her tan skin was glowing and her dark brown hair shined in the sunlight. Half her face was covered with her arm and yet it was still very easy to tell how pretty she was beneath it.

Pool water splashed at my feet drawing my attention away from the girl. Sean had jumped in and was now resurfacing, pushing his hair back out of his face. Knox was leaning against the bar, sipping on his drink while Liam talked to him.

Thinking for a split second, I made my decision. I had come here to swim so swimming is what I shall do.

I quickly pulled my tank top off and dropped it next to my towel before stepping out of my shorts and doing the same. I could feel his gaze burning into me again but I didn't let myself think about it before I turned and jumped into the water.

Its effect was instant, successfully cooling me off as the sun shined brightly overhead.

I, too, pushed my hair out of my face, gasping for air once I broke the surface. Treading water, my eyes found Sean a few feet away doing the same. Normally I would look away, avoiding prolonged eye-contact at all costs but Knox had brought something out of me earlier - something that wanted to test the limits a bit.

"Do you know how to float on your back?" I asked Sean.

His eyes glinted with mischief - as if he understood exactly what I was trying to do - as he studied my face before responding, "Do you not?"

"I've always wanted to learn." I shrugged, trying to calm my rapidly beating heart.

I knew Knox was listening - knew he wouldn't let anything bad happen to me - but I also hadn't really thought through my words before I spoke them. Sean seemed to be looking for trouble just as much as I was as he drew closer to me.

"Lean back and let your legs float up from underneath you." Sean said, his voice a bit quieter now that he was so close. "I'll hold you up."

I gulped, licking my dry lips. Glancing between his eyes, I knew he meant no harm but I couldn't help the growing panic that tightened my chest. I ignored it the best I could, closing my eyes as I leaned back and did just as he said. His hand met my back, nearly making me gasp in surprise.

I held my breath as he helped me push up, water filling my ears and teasing the outline of my body as I laid half above the water and half below it. Slowly my panic ebbed away and a smile started to grace my face.

It lasted all of two seconds before a hand gripped my ankle and pulled me out of Sean's hold. Gasping, my eyes flew open as I was yanked into Knox's chest. He didn't say a word as he dragged me out of the water and pulled me through a side door of the house that revealed a bathroom.

My wide eyes took in Knox's furious face as he closed the door behind us. I bit my lip, taking a step away from him. Maybe intentionally trying to push his buttons wasn't such a good, fully thought-through idea after all.

"Annie," His voice was low and controlled - holding back, "tell me what the fuck that was." He said, stalking forward as I matched his every step to back up until my back hit the wall, his arms instantly coming up to cage me in.

"I-I wanted to learn how to float." I whispered, my voice trembling slightly - stemming just as much from nerves as from excitement.

"And you asked Sean to teach you?" He all but seethed, "You wanted Sean to get that close to you - put his hands on you?" His eyes burned furiously, his stare not wavering from me once.

I squirmed slightly, his gaze too intense. "No." I confessed, forcing the word out.

"So why the fuck didn't you ask me?"

"I-I wanted to make you jealous." I whispered, turning my head away from him in total embarrassment at the confession. Tears stung at the back of my eyes, threatening to mortify me even further.

Knox let out an unamused breath as he clicked his tongue. His hand came up to grip my face, squeezing my cheeks between his fingers as he forced me to look at him again. "Such a fucking brat." Knox whispered more to himself than to me. "Baby, you don't have to fight so hard for my attention, you already have all of it. Say the word and I'll give you everything you ask for."

His eyes danced across my face - waiting. His chest rose and fell rapidly, brushing against me as he breathed. I should be scared - should be freaking out - but I wasn't. All I wanted right now was Knox - all of him.

"Please." I whispered out breathily, a pathetic plead.

Before I could blink, Knox's hand was threaded through my wet hair, gripping the back of my neck as his lips devoured mine. My hands came up to his chest, fisting his t-shirt between my fingers. Barely giving me a second to breathe, Knox kissed me like a starved man - hungry and unrelenting.

When I was able to break away, gulping down air, his lips trailed down my jaw and neck. He nipped at my neck, letting his tongue swirl over the red area his teeth left behind. I shuddered in his grasp, digging my nails into his shoulders.

Pulling away with one last kiss, I nearly whimpered at the loss of contact. Knox wasn't done, though. A small smirk quirked his lips at my noise before he turned me around and lifted me so I was laying on my stomach atop the bathroom counter.

I hissed at the contact of the cold countertop against my burning hot skin.

Knox leaned over, his hand cupping me as he asked, "You want me to touch you, baby?"

My eyes glazed over, my mind filling with fog. Nodding my head, my breath hitched as his thumb gently rubbed circles against my still clothed core.

"Words, Annie." He ordered.

"Yes, please." I gasped out, my thighs clenching around his hand.

"Such good manners." He praised, toying with the edge of my bathing suit bottoms before pushing them to the side. My breath caught in my throat as the cold air hit my most sensitive area, already drenched with need.

He stroked one finger up and down my center lazily as I squirmed against him. I was already panting - desperate for more.

"So wet for me already and I've barely touched you." Knox hummed, bringing his other hand up to palm my ass - spreading me even more before him.

I choked on my moan as he slid a single finger inside me. "This is mine." Knox grit out, "This pussy belongs to me. Only I can touch it, right, baby?"

My eyes rolled to the back of my head as he pumped me slowly, grazing his finger along my walls. His thumb drew circles against my clit, drawing out another shudder from me.

"Tell me." Knox demanded, his fingers stilling where they were. I gasped, my legs shaking.

"It's yours." I forced out the words, choking on them as he continued pumping me once again. He added a second digit, forcing me to stretch around him.

"What's mine?" He teased, rubbing my clit faster as he added more pressure.

"This pussy - it's yours." I moaned.

Knox pumped faster, covering my mouth with his other hand as I shook with my release. My entire body slumping as I finished, Knox now pulling out before bringing his fingers to my mouth.

"Open." He said.

I opened my mouth and closed it around his two fingers, sucking off my climax as he watched me with hooded eyes.

"Good girl." He groaned. "My good girl."

17

- -

I continued to lay, still panting, on the counter for several minutes as Knox cleaned me and set my bikini bottoms back into place. I nearly whimpered at the contact of the cloth against my now extra sensitive skin. He then helped me stand back up, my legs slightly unsteady beneath me as they still slightly shook - only making Knox smirk in satisfaction.

Liam and Sean shot knowing looks between them when Knox and I had walked out of that bathroom. I tried my best to stifle the rising embarrassment and played innocent - hoping to avoid addressing it at all costs. Thankfully, neither of them said anything when we joined them.

If I felt clingy before, it was only more pronounced now. I now sat perched on Knox's lap as he sat on the bar stool, his fingers lazily grazing my hip in small circles. I leaned my back against his chest, my body heavy and tired as I sunk against him.

Each blink gradually became more and more of a struggle, my eyes desiring nothing more than to stay closed. My breathing evened out and grew heavier as I snuggled even more into him. I was seconds away from unconsciousness when his chest rumbled against me as he spoke.

"Nah. I've been thinking about dropping out. Competing hasn't been worth it lately." He said, replying to whatever they were talking about.

My eyes blinked rapidly. I had been so zoned out, I was at a complete loss. I would have thought he was talking about school if he hadn't just mentioned something about competing. But I didn't give it much thought before letting my eyes flutter closed again.

"Some of us don't have that luxury." Sean grit out. My eyes shot open at the sound of his fist hitting the counter. Knox's fingers stopped their gentle stroking, now gripping my hip tightly.

"I didn't say I wouldn't help you out." Knox spat back, sitting up straighter and bringing me with him.

Sean scoffed, looking away as he sucked his teeth. "I thought you of all people would know how much I fucking need this."

I glanced back and forth between the counter top and Sean - not sure completely where to look.

Knox tensed beneath me, considering Sean's words. "One more - I'll do one more but then that's it. I can't keep risking my fucking neck for this shit." He dragged his hand down his face, letting out an irritated sigh.

Sean nodded his head, his jaw still tight with anger but he relented nonetheless.

I shifted against Knox, my mind working as I tried to figure out what they could possibly be talking about. Whatever it was, it sounded dangerous and I didn't like the sound of it. I was tempted to ask but I also wasn't sure it was something I would want to actually know. Maybe I would ask Knox when it was just him and I again - when he wasn't just involved in a slightly heated discussion.

I shifted again, trying to look behind me towards the pool. Knox abruptly brought his hand up to grip my face, forcing me look at him as he whispered, "Move against me one more time, Annie, and I'll take you back to that bathroom and fuck you with more than just my finger." He said lowly, his words dripping with promise.

I sucked in a sharply, fighting the urge to writhe in his hold.

"Can we go swim now?" I asked softly, biting my lip as I tried to ignore the warm sensation that spread through me at his words.

I collapsed on my bed a couple hours later, having just showered all the chlorine off of me after the pool. But not even the shower could wash away the feeling that Knox's hands left imprinted all over my body.

My thighs clenched as I thought back to the bathroom and forced myself to take a steadying breath.

I had never done anything like that before - never touched myself or let anyone else touch me like that before. My mind blocked out how far the boy who assaulted me had gotten but I knew for certain that it hadn't felt anything like this.

Knox's hands were soft and caressed me so gently, I could've melted there in his arms.

I itched for more every time my mind drew back to that moment. And Knox seemed to know it too. Every look he gave me caused a burning heat to pool in the pit of my stomach and had my body tensing with desire.

I felt insatiable and so so much more attached.

I pouted the whole way when Knox eventually drove me home. Maybe he was right to call me a brat when I acted like this.

I was already camped out on the couch, flipping through channels when Serena came home with a big smile on her face. After setting her stuff down on the counter and taking her shoes off, she plopped down next to me on the couch and let out a content sigh.

"Pizza?" She asked, turning her head to look at me with a grin.

"Pizza." I nodded, grinning right back.

It had been a long day - apparently for both of us.

"How was your meeting?" I asked after Serena finished ordering our food.

"It went well. I'm hoping everything continues to go smoothly - a promotion soon would be nice." She hummed before turning her attention on me, "And what did you do all day?" She asked.

I cleared my throat, thinking. I knew I had to tell her about Knox and now was as good a time as any - I couldn't continue avoiding it. If anybody deserved to know, it would be Serena.

"The friend I made invited me to go swimming." I said, slowly easing into parts of the truth.

"Oh?" Serena held back her grin but her twinkling eyes gave away her excitement.

"His name is Knox..." I tried to ignore Serena's eyebrows shooting up in shock as I continued, "He's been helping me through all of my classes and he is also who I've been hanging out with after school - him and his two friends." I gulped, glancing nervously between Serena and my fidgeting fingers.

"Wow, Annie. That's incredible." Serena breathed out.

"He's really kind to me. I feel how much he understands me - it's comforting." I muttered, suddenly feeling shy at how overwhelming my gratitude for him was becoming.

"I am so proud of you for coming out of your shell - for continuing to pushing yourself. But also for being authentic...If Knox has been so kind to you, then I'm glad that you have him as a friend." Serena smiled warmly.

My heart nearly burst in my chest as it swelled with so much love for Serena. Emotion lodged itself in my throat as tears stung at the back of my eyes, with me trying to force both of them down.

Knox's pov

I drove back to Liam's after dropping Annie off. Her attitude in the car had started to piss me off and it was a struggle holding back from fixing it but she had already taken enough for the day - no matter how badly I wanted to pull her over my knee.

She was a lot more to handle than I had originally bargained for and for as frustrating as it was, I was also grateful for it.

Using Sean to make me jealous - I scoffed. The worst part was that it had worked. Beneath that innocent face and those doe-eyes was a sneaky, scheming girl. And the brat was all mine.

Really it was Sean's stupid smirk that had set me off. He knew it would too which had to be exactly why he did it. If he wasn't my friend and I didn't trust his true intentions, I wouldn't have been so forgiving.

I let out a puff of smoke as I passed the joint back to Liam - grateful Annie couldn't stick around for this part. I couldn't, wouldn't, smoke around her. Her innocence and curiosity would make it impossible. Regardless, I couldn't bring myself to be like that in her presence anyways - it didn't feel right.

I sunk further into the cushions of the couch - my body finally fully relaxing for the first time the entire day. I shut my eyes, humming in satisfaction.

"Annie's got claws after all, huh?" Liam laughed, nudging me as he took a hit.

"Shut up." I grumbled before allowing myself to nod off.

18

Knox was sprawled on his back, sideways across my bed, staring at his phone. He had been like that for almost an hour, practically unmoving. Occasionally he would let out a snort-like breath of air and then go back to complete silence.

I kept glancing up at him every few seconds from my spot on the floor. I couldn't stop myself - his presence was all too consuming.

Textbooks and notebooks laid open all around me. I was trying to get some of our homework done and it was proving to be more difficult than I thought. Knox obviously wasn't helping - in fact, it was quite distracting.

He had texted me this morning that he wanted to see me and I couldn't come up with any valid reason to say no - not that I wanted to anyways. When I asked Serena, she smiled so hard I was concerned for the wellbeing of her cheeks.

That being said, I was grateful she hadn't grilled him the second he walked in the door. She had promised she wouldn't bombard him but even then, she was all too happy to introduce herself. Like expected, Knox was polite and happy to meet her, but I couldn't help myself from feeling embarrassed about the whole interaction.

I had dragged a grinning Knox away and up to my room as fast as possible - still leaving the door open.

He didn't seem to mind that I was doing school work, though. He looked content enough to just lounge around. He wasn't even really doing anything that could be deemed as distracting, not even shifting around much at all. Yet I still couldn't stop my eyes from continuously sliding over to look at him.

"You've been on the same page for 10 minutes." He said, his matter-of-fact voice making me jump in my skin. He didn't turn his head as he spoke, continuing to scroll on his phone.

"I-I..." I sputtered, startled and confused at how he knew that if I hadn't seen him look.

A smirk grew at the corner of his lips making me flush.

"At least I'm doing my work." I grumbled under my breath, refocusing on the textbook I indeed hadn't touched for over 10 minutes now.

"Don't worry about me, Annie, baby. I already finished it all." Knox grinned, his eyes sparkling as he finally turned to look at me.

I narrowed my eyes at him, frowning, "And you've been letting me struggle by myself this whole time?"

I let out an annoyed puff of air.

"All you had to do was ask." He laughed as he sat up, sliding his phone back into his pocket.

"Please..." I pouted.

Standing up, he made his way over to me. "A kiss per question." He said.

"Huh?" I furrowed my brows, looking up at him from beneath my lashes.

"That's my price. Every answer I give you, you give me a kiss." He restated as he sat down next to me and leaned his back against the wall.

I flushed, nervously tucking my hair behind my ear. "Okay." I whispered, swallowing down my nervous excitement. No matter how many times I've kissed him now, I wasn't sure I'd ever get used to it.

Even just having him this close to me was enough to have my heart racing and my mind turning to mush.

Knox looked at me expectantly, gesturing his hand out in the direction of all the papers strewn about.

"Oh." I flushed again in embarrassment as I reached for the closest one.

History - my worst subject by far. I was horrible at remembering events accurately as I always conflated important historical events together. And don't even get me started on the dates. My eyes darted around the page, taking in the first question.

"In what ways did political and religious liberties expand after the Revolution?" I asked, my heart still beating rapidly as I spared a glance at Knox.

He raised a brow, not saying a single word. I blinked and tilted my head - confused. A ghost of a smile played on his lips as he rolled his eyes before reaching for me. I gasped as he loosely took hold of the side of my neck, pulling me into him as he claimed my lips. I melted into him immediately, nearly moaning as my lips moulded against his.

His tongue swiped at my bottom lip, his hand moving to hold a fist of my hair as he tugged slightly - eliciting a soft gasp from me so he could slip his tongue in my mouth. I tried my best to keep up as his tongue greedily filled my mouth but found myself gasping for air as he pulled away a few moments later.

I stared up at him, my mouth slightly agape as I panted softly.

His thumb swiped at my bottom lip, tugging on it as he spoke, "It democratized freedom and moved people toward religious toleration."

"Huh?" I gaped, completely distracted by the hand that had stopped fisting my hair and had begun gently massaging my scalp.

"Write it down, baby." He whispered a breath from my lips, teasing me.

I blinked and then blinked again before abruptly pulling away, his hands releasing me. I scribbled his words under the first question, gripping my pencil so tight I could have snapped it if I was any stronger.

Knox loosed an amused breath from beside me, no doubt the smirk having returned to his face.

Half an hour and only four questions later, my face was burning and my heart still wasn't under control. Knox, however, was just as calm and collected as always - save for the mischievous twinkle in his eyes.

I glanced down at my half-finished paper and let out a frustrated puff. The sun was beginning to set outside my window and I still had other subjects to finish before going to school tomorrow. At this rate, I was going to be up all night trying to get everything done.

"You're - You're doing this on purpose." I whined, frowning.

Knox breathed out a laugh, a teasing smile overtaking his face. "What? What could I possibly be doing on purpose, baby?" He asked.

"You're making sure I don't finish my homework in time." I glared.

Maybe it was wrong to let out my frustration and anxiety out on Knox but I wasn't totally wrong. He was making me take longer to complete my assignments than it would have taken me if I was on my own.

Knox scoffed incredulously, arguing, "Wha - Annie, I've been giving you the answers."

"After continuously distracting me!"

Knox laughed again. "You're right, baby. I'm sorry. I keep letting myself get carried away." He smiled, reaching to slip the paper out of my hands. Taking my pencil, he focused his attention on filling in the rest of the answers before passing it back to me.

"Forgive me?" He asked in a mumble as he kissed my cheek.

I nodded my head, biting my lip to keep myself from further derailing us from getting my work done.

The knock on the door a second later had me glad I did, too. I snapped my head over to see Serena standing in the doorway, smiling at us where we sat.

"Knox, are you staying for dinner?" She asked.

Knox smiled back, "Oh, thank you. I would love to but I really can't."

I fiddled with my pencil, avoiding looking at him as he answered. I couldn't help the disappointment from seeping in. Obviously I knew that Knox wouldn't be able to stay with me at all times but that didn't stop me from wishing he could.

"Okay, maybe next time." Serena smiled gently before retreating back down the stairs and out of sight.

Silence consumed the air around us for several moments until Knox cleared his throat. He left a soft kiss beneath my ear before whispering, "I'll see you tomorrow, okay, baby?"

I nodded, shooting him a feeble smile before watching him get up and leave.

19

- -

I did not, in fact, see Knox the next day.

I sat on my usual bench, still waiting for him to show up well after the first bell hand rung. Not a single other person was in sight as I sat there. I waited and waited - even texting Knox twice without receiving a single response. Neither Liam nor Sean had made any appearance either.

I couldn't call Serena to pick me up - I would be too embarrassed to admit that I couldn't walk into school without Knox at my side. I may have been getting better but that felt completely dependent on his presence and there was no way I could admit that to Serena without worrying her even more.

And with Knox not answering my texts, I had no choice other than to walk home.

My legs were stiff and my eyes glistened with tears the entire way home. Not only had he not answered me and not warned me in any way that he wouldn't be at school, but he had told me just yesterday that he would see me today.

He lied.

He still didn't show up Tuesday. Nor did he show up on Wednesday. By the time Thursday morning came, I didn't bother getting ready to even attempt seeing if he would be at school this time.

Serena knew I was coming back home immediately - skipping all my classes. At first, I was afraid to admit that the reason was because Knox wasn't with me but I couldn't lie to her when she had asked me so directly. She seemed to understand - or at least tried to. She honestly didn't say much, her face giving away none of her thoughts but she didn't argue when I continued to stay home.

I was grateful when Wendy had to cancel our normal session on Wednesday. She had come down with something and didn't want to risk it getting worse nor giving it to any of her patients. I felt more than relieved to know that I wouldn't have to admit to her that I was struggling with Knox's absence right now.

I spent my time at home fairly unproductively in all honesty. I traveled back and forth between the couch and my bed. I did manage to get all my homework done and I kept up with the assignments my teachers posted online, but I didn't do much else.

I rolled out of bed Friday morning feeling more sluggish than usual.

I had slept well and gone to bed at a reasonable hour, but after this entire week of doing practically nothing, I was starting to feel like a zombie.

I trudged down the stairs, Serena having left already, and went into the kitchen to make myself some chocolate milk.

I had been standing at the counter, sipping on my milk while staring out the kitchen window absentmindedly for not too long when a loud knock on the front door sounded through the house.

I frowned, still clutching my glass of milk as I slowly made my way over.

Peaking out the peep-hole, my eyes widened. My pulse immediately sky-rocketed, my palms grew slick, and my stomach churned. I wretched open the door, revealing none other than the boy who I'd been agonizing over all week.

And if I was being honest, Knox did not look himself. He had dark bags under his eyes as if he hadn't slept most of the week. His hair looked like he had been relying on just his fingers to comb through it and his eyes didn't have their usual light.

He looked like a shadow of himself.

"Knox?" I asked, shifting between my feet as I took in his appearance.

I wasn't sure exactly how I was supposed to be feeling in this moment. All week I had gone between feeling sad and mad, frustrated and confused at his surprise absence and overall radio silence. As much as I was expecting to still feel that way when seeing him again, even if part of me still is upset, I was also excited that he was finally in front of me again.

But, even then, something seemed to be seriously wrong and for that, I couldn't help feeling truly worried.

"Can I come in?" Knox asked, frowning.

I nodded, stepping to the side to let him pass over the threshold before closing the door behind him. I led him into the kitchen before rinsing out my glass and leaving it in the sink.

Knox leaned down with his elbows on the counter, letting his face fall into his hands.

"Knox..." I called, tentatively, "what's wrong?" I stepped next to him, using every bit of control I had to not reach out and touch him.

Knox dragged his hands down his face before turning to look at me. A sad smile tugged at the corner of his mouth.

I furrowed my brows in concern before gently taking his hand and leading him to the couch and plopping down. We sat together in silence for several moments. Knox wrapped his arm around my waist, pulling me flush against his side as he sighed.

"I didn't mean to disappear like that." He finally said, frowning before continuing, "I just - I got into a fight with my parents - nothing crazy unusual. It just got a bit ugly." He shrugged, trying to play off the hurt that I could still see lingering in his eyes.

"I'm sorry." I whispered, leaning further into him.

A fight with his parents stressing him out to the point that he looked like this was the last thing I expected. If this was something that was a common occurrence for him too, I couldn't even imagine how hurt he must really feel on the inside.

"No, I'm sorry. I should of texted you. I just went to Liam's and stayed there for a few days but I wasn't someone you would've wanted to be around." Knox said, tucking a strand of my hair behind my ear.

I unconsciously leaned into his touch, relishing in it after his long absence. "What do you mean?" I licked my dry lips, frowning again.

Knox loosed a deep breath, "Just didn't want you to see me like that - that's all, baby. I still should have texted you."

"I was really upset..." I admitted, trailing off as I remembered how much I had cried from the confusion I felt this past week.

"I know, baby. I'm sorry. It won't happen again." Knox promised as he lifted me slightly, pulling me over to straddle his lap. His hands met my hips, the touch warm and gentle.

"I missed you." I whispered, pouting slightly as I started toying with the fabric of his shirt between my fingers.

I could feel the heat of Knox studying my face for several moments before he pulled me flush against his chest.

"Let me make it up to you." He urged quietly, leaving a trail of light kisses down my jaw. Tangling his hand in my hair, he tugged just hard enough to expose more of my neck to his lips as he continued his path.

My lips parted and my hands met his chest to brace myself.

A loud whine escaped my mouth as he bit the skin of my neck, immediately licking and kissing the spot better. My hands clenched, fisting his shirt between my fingers as he repeated his actions again in a different spot and again somewhere else. His lips acting as a sweet torture that sent my mind into a frenzy.

Pulling away, he released his hold on my hair before bringing his hand around to loosely grip my neck.

I drew in a sharp breath, his fingers flexing around my throat. His eyes were dark and predatory - his tongue darting out to lick his lips. I gulped, feeling the weight of his hand with the movement.

I could feel arousal pooling between my legs - the gnawing ache becoming almost unbearable. My hips twitched against him, the slight friction creating no relief.

The look in Knox's eyes flared at my movement. I squirmed, my lower half throbbing against the fabric of his jeans. He squeezed my throat in warning when I started to move again. A small whimper passed my lips - desperate and needy.

"Knox...please..." I whined out, begging.

A low groan left his throat as he quickly flipped me to lay on my back atop the couch. His hand landed next to my head, holding him up as he hovered over me. His other hand instantly went to the silk shorts of my pajamas, moving them and my cotton panties aside.

I barely felt the cool air hitting me as circled my heat before plunging two fingers inside me. I gasped, my body writhing beneath him. I clenched around his fingers as they relentlessly pumped in and out of me. Knox captured my lips with his own, muffling my moan as he added a third finger. His thumb met my clit a moment later. The combination of the three inside me and the fourth steadily rubbing against me had me unraveling in a matter of moments.

I laid gasping for air, my body shaking as he pulled away.

His eyes roamed over my panting form as he sat back. His hands undoing the button and zipper of his jeans, his eyes still wild with lust.

I watched with wide eyes as his length sprang out before me - big, hard, and waiting.

I shuddered as I watched Knox start stroking it before me, using my climax that still glistened on his hand as lubricant. His other hand snaked up my stomach, forcing my silk tank top up, revealing my breasts that were heavy and full with desire.

Knox groaned again, his dick twitching in his hand as he stroked it faster. His other hand squeezed one of my breasts, digging his fingers into my flesh.

I squirmed against him, my breathing coming out in soft pants. I could feel the ache coming back and growing even stronger than before.

Knox brushed the tip of his dick against the folds of my opening, coating it with more of my arousal. My eyes rolled to the back of head, my back arching off the couch.

"Fuck...not yet." Knox whispered under his breath, more to himself than to me.

I silently thanked him. Even if it felt so good and I wouldn't stop him if he were to fill me up right now, I knew I wasn't ready for all that yet.

He pulled his length away from me a second later, his thighs tensing and his hand slowing down. His release now coated my bare stomach as he let out one final groan.

20

"Are you ever going to tell me what you and your parents argued about?" I asked Knox a few days later.

I sat criss-crossed at the top of my bed, facing him as he laid on his back with his crossed arms covering his closed eyes. He had still been as off as he had been when I first saw him a few days before. He continuously tried to play it off since then - pretend nothing was bothering him - but I could tell.

"You wouldn't like it." His voice was gruff and partially muffled by his arms.

I frowned, looking down at my hands as they fiddled in my lap.

"But it's been bothering you..." I whispered, trailing off.

I couldn't help feeling slightly discouraged.

I had confided in Knox before and I couldn't help wishing he would do the same. Even if it was an unfair expectation, I wanted him to know that I'm here for him and I wanted him to feel comfortable telling me how he's feeling. Obviously I don't want to force him but it was a bit hurtful that he was so resistant.

"Is it what you've been arguing about with Sean and Liam?" I pried further, my voice timid as I was afraid of crossing a line.

Ever since our pool day at Liam's, the air between them all has still been filled with tension. I frequently thought back to their conversation that I still failed to understand. I tried filling in the blanks but could never manage to fit the pieces together.

I had grown hyper aware of the tense and challenging looks that the three boys shot at each other throughout the school day. They weren't doing a very good job at hiding them even if they were good at hiding the reason behind it.

Knox sighed and dragged a hand down his face.

"Annie..." Knox groaned, "I appreciate your concern but I'm trying to protect you from this fucking mess."

"Please just let me be there for you." I pleaded under my breath, my last attempt at cracking his shell.

I held his eye as he studied me before he looked away and sat back up. He didn't look at me again, instead leaning over with his elbows resting on his knees.

"Liam, Sean, and I all compete in street races." Knox finally confessed.

My eyebrows shot up. Out of all things he could have said, this was the last thing I had expected.

"At first we started out cause it was fun for us. I mean fast cars, money, and the rush of doing something illegal..." He paused, sighing before continuing, "I guess it just became a habit. But I was starting to get tired of it and maybe Liam was a bit too - even if he'd never admit it. I mean the money has always been a plus but it's not something I need that badly - not as bad as Sean. His mom got sick last year and it's been really hard on their whole family. Racing earns him a lot more than working minimum wage would and having all three of us race makes it more likely at least one of us will win something. We usually split it evenly between us after."

Knox sighed again, finally turning his head to look at me. "As for my parents - my relationship with them is...complicated. They know about the racing and they definitely don't like it. That used to make me only want to do it more but now I think it'd be easier if I just stop."

"But then Sean..." I filled in, frowning as my mind worked to wrap around the predicament that has been plaguing Knox.

"But then Sean doesn't win as often as me - or even as often as Liam - so he'd be losing the money he needs." Knox finished.

I sat absorbing his words for what felt like endless minutes. Picking between saving his friendship or saving his relationship with his parents couldn't be an easy choice. I certainly didn't envy Knox's position.

"I'm really sorry." I offered, trying and failing to think of anything else to say that would make this situation better.

Knox shrugged, "I promised one more race. We'll figure it out after that."

I nodded, stilling wringing my hands in my lap.

"You're not upset about the racing?" Knox asked a second later, his head tilting to the side. A small spark of vulnerability danced in his eyes before it was gone.

I loosed a breath, thinking for only a moment before shaking my head. "No...It makes me nervous, but it's your choice."

I could visibly see some of the tension release from his shoulders as I spoke. He laid down on his back again, his entire body instantly much more relaxed.

"When is the race?" A slight gnawing grew in the pit of my stomach as I built up the courage to ask.

"Next Saturday." Knox said, blowing the word out in a breath.

"Can I come?" I asked, speaking the words quickly - before I could have time to hesitate and stop myself from speaking them entirely.

Knox stilled, the steady rise and fall of his chest paused for a long beat.

"No." He said a moment later, his tone firm and forceful.

"But why." I pouted slightly.

"It's not a place for you, Annie. It's not happening." He ground out. He sat up now, tugging me by my leg to pull me to his side.

I squeaked, "Bu-"

"It's crowded. Most people there are boys. And I won't be with you." Knox cut me off, taking hold of my face. His eyes were dark as they flared, daring me to continue arguing with him.

"I promise I'll be good." I pleaded out in a whisper. Jutting out my bottom lip and putting on my best puppy-dog eyes, I all but begged.

Knox's jaw twitched, his fingers flexed on my face. His eyes roamed around my face - he was thinking.

"You will do everything I say." He finally ground out through his teeth.

My eyes widened as I tried to nod my head but his hold on my face firmly kept me still.

"I have a couple friends you can watch with who will keep you safe. But I mean it, everything I say. If you so much as blink wrong, I can promise you won't like what I'll do."

I gulped and tried nodding but was yet again prevented.

"Words." Knox all but ordered.

"I will do everything you say...I promise." I breathed.

Knox hummed, brushing his lips against mine in a ghost of a kiss before pulling away and releasing my face.

He laid back down, once again shutting his eyes as I gulped. My heart was fighting to break out of my chest and my mind was shooting all over the place. As I sat there trying to comprehend what I use got myself into, I found myself wondering how bad it could truly be.

21

"Annie." Serena called out from the bottom of the stairs.

"Coming." I shouted back, leaving my comfortable position on my bed.

I walked down the steps and found Serena leaning against the counter in the kitchen, seemingly reading something on her phone. I stopped in the doorway, fiddling my fingers as I waited for her to speak.

My anxiety had been getting worse as the week went on. The anticipation for Knox's race was beginning to consume me. Having convinced him to let me go was one thing but actually going was something else entirely.

We hadn't even been able to spend as much time together as he and Liam and Sean had all been going to practice and prepare after school each day.

Knowing the race would be tomorrow, the nerves were eating me up.

I knew how dangerous this race was going to be for me to attend but it had to be so much worse for the three of them - they would be the ones actually in the cars. I couldn't stand the thought of something happening to any one of them.

I gulped at the thought, shifting on my feet as I still stood waiting for Serena to say something.

"I need to talk to you about something." Serena broke the silence, still not glancing up from whatever she was now typing. Her voice was monotone - giving absolutely nothing away.

What was the likelihood she could hear my thoughts? What if she had somehow found out what I was planning to do - planning to go see? She surely wouldn't stand for it. She probably wouldn't let me see Knox ever again - he'd be considered too much of a bad influence. Serena would lose her mind and I'd subsequently lose mine too.

I couldn't breathe. The panic that gripped my chest already had too tight a hold, I couldn't fight it back.

"My boss invited me to have dinner with her and her family tonight..."

And just like that, I could breathe again.

"I want to say that of course you are welcome to come along and I would obviously love to bring you with me. I do just want you to know that they have a teenage son who will be there and I don't want to put you in a situation you're not comfortable with." Serena finished, finally looking up as sent me a warm smile.

My shoulders relaxed instantly. If this was all she wanted to talk about, I could deal with that.

It was so relieving, in fact, that it took me a second before I realized she was waiting for me to answer her unspoken question.

"Oh..." I paused, blinking a few times as I thought about my answer. "I have been making progress..." I paused again, frowning.

"Of course you have and I'm so proud of you. But there is still no pressure." Serena assured.

"I-I think I can do it. I'd like to do it." I wanted to be there to support Serena. She had been working so hard to get promoted at work and being invited to have dinner with her boss and her boss's family was a big thing. I definitely needed to be there to support her - to show up for her just as she has been showing up for me.

Serena beamed, bringing me into a big hug before pulling away again. "Thank you, Annie. Go started getting ready. We'll leave at 5." She gushed, ushering me away.

The side effects of my previously raging anxiety left me still slightly dazed as I went through the routine of getting ready for this dinner. I moved around with hardly any knowledge of what I was doing, letting my muscle memory control me as my mind wandered.

I thought of Serena's boss and if her son was in my grade, if he went to my school, if I would know him. I shoved those last thoughts to the back of my mind as quickly as I could - that would be worst case scenario. I also thought of Knox and the race, and whether or not he was going to be practicing tonight.

I thought about sending him a text but before I knew it, Serena was calling that it was time to go.

The drive to Serena's boss's house was long, taking us clear across town. Serena and I lived in a nice neighborhood with nice homes and nice people but that's all it really was - nice. Nice and very average.

This part of town was anything but average.

These were homes with long, twisty drive ways, gates that had special codes and iron tops, manicured lawns adorned with sparkling fountains.

I was only slightly comforted in knowing I had at least dressed up a little bit - even if I did still stick out like a sore thumb in my white ballet flats and pink-flowered mini dress.

We waited at their giant oak front door that could've easily spanned two floors for only a few seconds before it was pried open by the woman herself.

"Serena." She smiled warmly, opening the door further so that we could squeeze inside - not that it was much of a squeeze.

"Emily." Serena smiled back with equal vigor.

"You must be Annie." Emily smiled, shutting the door behind us.

I nodded, mustering up the best smile I could.

"Well, Tyler should be done getting the table all the set up. The casserole is almost done so - oh there he is. Tyler, show them to the dining room. Please take any seats you like." Emily smiled briefly once more before quickly making her way back to the kitchen.

My eyes shot to Tyler as he entered the doorway. He was very tall and broad but not nearly as built as to be expected for someone of his size. His stare was cold and I instantly found myself more interested in looking down at my feet.

He gestured at us to follow him into the dining room. It was no less extravagant inside the house than it was outside and the dining room was no exception, even if it was only set for four people.

Serena and I took our seats next to each other. I smoothed my dress as I sat, unable to help myself from fidgeting as Tyler took the seat across from me. He still had yet to say a word and it was beginning to unnerve me.

I nearly gasped as the pant of his knee brushed me under the table. I jerked my legs away, leaning as far back in my chair as I could. My eyes met his in complete shock, his eyes twinkling under the warm light of the chandelier.

Emily brought the casserole out a mere matter of moments later, although it did little to distract me. I could hardly stomach taking a few bites with the nausea that slowly stirred in me.

Emily and Serena quickly took up conversation, droning on about the firm and the many changes that are happening in the coming months. I was trying my best to listen actively, wanting to not come across as withdrawn as I felt, but it wasn't working.

Tyler's stare was burning into the side of my face.

His foot bumped into mine a second later, effectively making me spring out of my seat at the contact.

The loud screech of the dining chair moving had everyone's eyes falling on me. The quizzical glances and immediate silence indicating the death of a conversation was enough to send overwhelming waves of embarrassment through my system.

"Um-" I hesitated, clearing my throat as I wracked my brain for an excuse for my border-line rude behavior. "Sorry, I- Uh where is the bathroom?" I stammered out.

It was lame but it seemed to do that trick as understanding washed over Emily's features.

"Oh, it's just down the hall, dear. Tyler can show you." Emily waved her hand, gesturing at Tyler to stand up and lead the way.

This was the absolute last thing I wanted and if I knew it was going to lead to this, I would've tried to come up with some other excuse. Maybe I just thought I saw a mouse or I don't know, anything that meant I didn't have to be alone with this unnerving boy.

I didn't say that, though - couldn't say that. Instead, I nodded my head solemnly and followed him through the door and out of sight.

I wrung my hands together, trying my best to stop their shaking. I stayed a few paces behind him, trying to keep as much of my sanity as I could. I was grateful when he didn't speak a single word. He simply walked a steady pace before pointing to the bathroom door once we got there. I gave him an awkwardly forced half smile and shut the door, locking it the second it closed behind me.

I leaned my head against the wood for a brief moment, letting out a momentary sigh of relief. I then turned around to the sink before splashing my face with water. Looking at myself in the mirror, my skin was flushed and the panic was slowly beginning to fade into the background of my eyes. It was the best I could do for the moment.

I stood there, trying my best to regulate my breathing for a few more moments before turning back towards the door.

I wholeheartedly expected Tyler to have left the second I had shut the door a few minutes prior, but I was sorely mistaken.

There he stood, proudly leaning against the opposite wall as I stood in the bathroom doorway.

All the work I had just done felt as it had been tossed out of the window. My pulse was back to beating furiously and my breathing once again turned shallow.

"I've seen you before." He said, calmly. His voice washed over me, making the hair on the back of my neck stand up.

I gulped but didn't say anything.

"You seem like a good girl, Annie." He said again, standing up straighter now as he focused his full attention onto me. "I won't lie, Knox doesn't seem like such a good influence for you."

I scratched my arms as I brought them around my middle in a self-hug. My mouth was dry, any words I had were lodged in the back of my throat and were not moving any time soon.

"If I were you, I'd stay away. I'd hate to see you become a casualty."

My stomach turned over, and my body swayed slightly before I turned and hunched over the toilet.

22

I cried myself to sleep that night, my body shaking as I continuously sobbed. I tossed a turned, taking forever to fall asleep. Every turn I took, Tyler's threatening words followed me. I didn't know how he knew Knox and I didn't know what he had against him, but I did know becoming a "casualty" would not be a good thing for me.

Serena had taken me home immediately, ending the night much earlier than planned.

I felt absolutely horrible for causing her to miss out on such an important opportunity. The only thing I could do was hope that her boss, Emily, wouldn't hold it against her. It didn't seem like she would considering how friendly she was and how understanding she seemed when Serena explained the situation to her before we left, but you never know. Emily is the one that birthed Tyler of all people, so how much I could trust that she wouldn't hold it against Serena, I didn't know.

At some point I must have fallen asleep as I woke up to the harsh noise of my alarm, signaling my need to start getting ready for Knox to come over.

His race wasn't until tonight and I wouldn't need to start getting ready for it for several hours but Knox wanted to come over and spend the day relaxing with me. I wouldn't complain.

I showered, brushed my teeth, and got dressed with no real hurry. I did my best to hide the dark circles and red, puffiness of having cried for so long last night.

I debated with myself the entire time on whether I should tell Knox about what Tyler said or not. It felt like every second I was switching the answer in my mind. I knew that it was something Knox would want to know, assuming that Tyler was an actual threat, but I also didn't want to distract him and potentially stress him out before his race.

I was still debating with myself when the doorbell rung and I went to answer the door.

I swung the door open to meet a smiling Knox, wearing a plain black tee and dark jeans. The fit was simple and yet mouthwatering all the same.

"Baby." He greeted, grinning as he stepped inside.

"Hi." I whispered, getting goosebumps from the sound of his voice.

I shut the door, fighting down my blush as Knox greeted Serena.

"You two just hanging out?" Serena, asked smiling as she stood at the sliding glass door to the backyard.

"Yeah, nothing special." Knox laughed.

"Well, I'll be out gardening if you two need anything." She said, sending me a warm glance. I knew she was saying it to be polite to Knox, but deep down I knew she really meant it for me - to know I wasn't alone.

I sent her a grateful smile back before leading Knox up to my room and leaving my door cracked.

"Are you nervous?" I asked, taking a seat in the middle of my bed. I wrung my hands together as I watched Knox kick his shoes off next to my door.

"For the race? Nah." Knox brushed off, turning around and walking towards me.

"Not at all?" I asked, my eyes widening slightly in surprise.

"Nah." Knox affirmed as he kneeled on the edge of the bed, his hands taking hold of my legs to open them.

I gasped, confused for only a split second before he laid down between them, resting his head on my stomach - the action forcing me to lay on my back. His breath tickled my stomach as he laid a few gentle kisses to my belly before laying his head back down again.

I slowly ran my hands through his hair, massaging his head with my finger tips.

"Knox..." I started tentatively. I still wasn't entirely sure I should tell him but I needed to get it off my chest.

"Hm." He grunted, lazily bringing his hand to skim my side.

I drew in a sharp breath at the tickling sensation but continued nonetheless, "I - um... went out to dinner with Serena last night at her boss's house and uh - her boss's son was there..." I gulped, not sure how to explain really what happened.

Knox's hand stilled but he didn't move.

"His name is Tyler and he - uh he said that you're a bad influence on me and he doesn't want me to become a - a casualty." I fought the words out, my chest rising and falling rapidly from the build up of anxiety.

Knox lifted his head, leaning on the elbows on either side of my body as his eyes met mine.

"Tyler said I'm a bad influence on you and he doesn't want you to become a casualty..." Knox repeated slowly, his tone giving nothing of his thoughts away.

I gulped, nodding my head.

"And what did you say, Annie?" Knox asked, his eyes burning into mine.

"I-I didn't say anything...I was so scared, I threw up." My face burned with embarrassment at my admission but I had brought this conversation upon myself. I knew Knox wouldn't react very well and I didn't blame him for wondering what I may have said back to Tyler. If it were the other way around, I would've wanted to know how Knox responded.

Knox hummed, "He's who Liam and I got suspended for beating up. I'm not surprised he had something to say about it but you don't need to worry, baby. He won't do anything to you, I'll make sure of it." He promised.

I nodded, letting out a breath I didn't even know I had been holding.

"Who - um - who am I going to be watching the race with?" I asked, wanting to talk about anything other than Tyler now that I had gotten it off our chest.

"Liam's girl, Clarissa, and her brother. You'll like Clarissa, she's very out-going." Knox said.

"Is she the one who was napping when we were at Liam's for swimming?" I asked thinking back to a while ago.

Knox nodded before rolling off of me and standing up.

"And her brother?" I asked as I sat up to keep looking at him - my question about him not entirely clear, and yet Knox understood it just the same.

"Her brother is trustworthy and I wouldn't let you be around him if I didn't know that he would keep you safe." Knox assured confidently before he walked to my closet and slide the door open.

I nodded, my anxiety slowly ebbing away at the knowledge that Knox would do his best to always keep me safe.

"What are you doing?" I asked, my brows furrowing as he started shifting things around in my closet.

"Looking for something you can wear tonight." He answered, his back to me as he continued sifting through my clothes.

"I already know what I'm going to wear." I frowned, standing up and walking to my dresser before holding up my planned outfit.

Knox turned his head, glancing at the black clothing I held in my hands.

"Let me see you in it." He said as he took a seat at the edge of my bed.

My cheeks tinged pink as I tried and failed to think of a reason to say no. Instead, I walked into my bathroom and changed as quickly as I could. I wore a black, leather mini skirt and a cut, cropped black graphic tee of a nascar race. It was the best I could do considering I wasn't one to usually dress very "edgy" and I had no idea what dressing for a race like this would really look like.

I stepped out of the bathroom, Knox's eyes on me immediately.

"Absolutely not." Knox grumbled without hesitation.

"What?" I all but whined, "What's wrong with it?" I stepped closer to him, pouting.

Knox reached out to pull me over his lap, making me gasp in shock.

"What's wrong with it?" Knox scoffed, "This shit doesn't even cover your ass, Annie." Knox brought his hand down on my bum, the sound of the slap echoing in my room.

My mouth hung open, any and all words escaping me.

"You want your pretty pink panties on display for everyone all night?" Knox egged on, his hand now rubbing the area he had slapped.

"No." I gasped out. I tried bringing one of hands back to pull down my skirt but Knox swatted my hand away.

"So tempting." Knox hummed, sliding his hand over my panties and down my middle.

"Let me make you feel good, baby." Knox coaxed, earning a small nod from me a second later.

I shuddered under his touch, sucking in a deep breath. My eyes fluttered closed as he gently rubbed circles, eliciting a soft moan from my mouth.

Knox slowly slid my panties down, leaving me bare before him.

I moaned again, louder as he slid a finger inside me, curling slightly. I whined as he added a second, pumping me faster now. His other hand came down on my ass in another harsh slap. I choked on my gasp.

Knox groaned, slapping once more before massaging the area gently.

"I can't wait to have you wrapped around my cock." Knox groaned, filling me with a third finger.

I panted as he continued to pump me, the fingers of his other hand dug into my ass so hard I knew they would bruise. His thumb massaged my clit, successfully working me into a frenzy before I came, spasming all over his fingers.

I twitched as he pulled out of my heat, bringing his fingers to his mouth before licking them clean. I blushed at the action, still laid limp and panting in his lap.

"Maybe I am a bad influence on you after all." Knox teased, brushing a kiss against my temple.

23

An hour and a half later, I had changed into some dark wash jeans and one of Knox's hoodies that he had in his car.

Serena had left a few minutes before to have dinner at our elderly neighbor, Ms. Marbury's, house as she does every so often. She knew Knox and I were going out tonight but I may have fed her a teensy lie about it being for dinner and a late movie instead. The guilt was already weighing on my conscious seconds after we stepped foot out of my house.

I chewed on my bottom lip in thought the entire way Knox drove us to the race track.

"I shouldn't have agreed to bring you." Knox grunted more to himself than me as he squeezed my thigh.

I glanced at the side of his face before looking back out the window. I couldn't bring myself to argue with him. Even I was starting to second guess why I asked to come in the first place.

In no time at all, we pulled onto a gravel road just outside of town, startling me from my thoughts. My eyes widened as they met the crowd of cars filling the otherwise empty lot. A rope perimeter circled the track, a thin veil of separation from the growing crowd of people.

I took a deep shuttering breath as Knox pulled up next to a small group of cars away from the main crowd.

I glanced over to see Liam, Sean, and who I vaguely recognized as Clarissa standing next to who I could only assume was her brother.

Knox lightly gripped my face, refocusing my attention on his face. He brushed his thumb over my bottom lip, his eyes roaming my face for a few moments before he captured my mouth in a rough kiss. He gripped the back of my neck, forcing my mouth open with his tongue. I gasped, gripping his shirt in a tight fist as I tried to keep up with his feverish movements. Knox was rough, controlling, and conveyed every ounce of emotion he couldn't say with words.

Pulling away, Knox left me dazed as I struggled to catch my breath.

He didn't say a single word as he stepped out of the car before walking around to open my door to help me out. My legs shook slightly with nerves as I stepped out. I gripped the end of Knox's shirt as he wrapped an arm around me, pulling me into his side. Leading us over to everyone else, Knox greeted them with a short nod of his head.

"Knox-y-boy," Liam grinned, "didn't think you were gonna make it." He laughed.

"I couldn't resist." Knox rolled his eyes, brushing Liam's teasing off. "How're you, Clarissa?" He asked, drawing my eyes to the girl I had only seen before.

"Excited to see a good race," she laughed, her eyes twinkling. "You must be Annie?" She asked, turning her attention to me.

I straightened, realizing how pathetic I must've looked cowering into Knox's side. I nodded, offering her the best smile I could muster. "Nice to meet you," I waved awkwardly.

"Likewise," She beamed. "This is my brother, Titus. Not much of a talker but I'm sure you're used to that with this one." She teased, gesturing to Knox.

I nodded, my smile easing into more a natural one. "Tell me about it." I joked, earning me a light pinch in the side from Knox himself.

"We need to get in the line-up." Sean's voice cut through the ease I was starting to feel, send my heart-rate sky-rocketing.

Liam and Knox nodded. Liam sent each Clarissa and I a cheeky wink before turning to jog to his car.

Knox leaned down to my ear, whispering so only I could hear, "The race won't be long. I'll be back before you know it. Just stay with Clarissa and Titus and you'll be alright. Be good for me, baby." He nipped my ear, earning a small squeak from me before he turned back to his own car.

I was suddenly grateful he made me change as I looked back over at the large group of people surrounding the track. There was no way I'd be comfortable here while wearing anything like that. And now with Knox no longer anywhere near me, I couldn't have happier to be wearing his hoodie.

Clarissa linked her arm with mine, sending me a reassuring smile as if she noticed where my focus had gone.

"Titus and I usually watch from over there." She said, pointing to a turn in the track that was less surrounded than the start/finish line. "We don't really like to bother with squeezing through everyone." She waved her hand, brushing the crowd off before leading me off to where they wanted to watch from.

"How many races have you been too?" I asked softly, still struggling to reel in the anxiety that was clawing its way up my throat.

"Hmmm," she paused, "a fair few but I certainly don't go to every single one. It gets a bit boring if you go too often." She confessed. "Plus, I don't think Liam likes me coming all the time."

"Why?" I asked before I could stop myself. My cheeks tinged pink in embarrassment, "You don't have to tell me if you don't feel comfortable." I tried to remedy.

Clarissa smiled at me warmly, "My relationship with Liam is a bit complicated. We each like our independence and neither of us are really looking for anything serious. It's nice to support each other but I know he can feel suffocated when I show up too much. I don't mind, though. I like where we're at and I don't need nor want to be around him all the time." She chuckled, again waving her hand as if to brush the whole thing off.

I furrowed my brows, not understanding how she could be so okay with his lack of commitment. If Knox ever said he was feeling suffocated by my presence, I don't think I could ever get over that. Nevertheless, it wasn't my place to judge.

Clarissa's eye's twinkled at my expression. "I know - you and Knox have a very different type of relationship so I'm sure it must be weird to you."

"No - I, I'm not judging at all. It's just - I thought-" I frowned, failing to find the words to explain.

"I know, Annie. Don't worry." She laughed, "I love what you have with Knox but it's just not what I want right now. Maybe in a few years but trust me, I am perfectly content right now."

I smiled, nodding as we came to halt where the rope separated the track.

Clarissa was right in that nobody was really over here, giving the three of us a comfortable amount of space to watch the race in peace.

Clarissa stood next to me, eagerly watching the cars line up at the start. Titus stood a bit behind the both of us, nursing a can of beer - his eyes glazed over with what I could only assume was boredom.

I licked my lips nervously, eyes darting everywhere for Knox's car. I took a deep, shuddered breath as he pulled up near the middle of the pack. Loud cheering sounded from the crowd as the race was set to start.

I wrung my hands together, my eyes never leaving Knox's car as a loud horn sounded and they all took off.

A/N

HI EVERYONE!!! I know it's been a while and for that I am so so sorry!! I got side tracked with vacation and then my internet was out for a while so I feel out routine BUT I am back and I will be trying my best to get back on schedule. I am going to be moving over the next couple of week so if I am less consistent than expected, then I apologize in advance. I promise I am not abandoning anything, I am just juggling a lot right now. Thank you so so much for your continued patience and support. I love you all so much and I am so glad to be back !! <3

24

From the moment they took off, everything was chaos. The crowd's cheers had only intensified, a few people even threw empty cans out into the track. I shrunk back slightly, tensing at the reactions from the crowd.

Even though we were far away from where most of the crowd was, the track was small enough that you could watch the entire ring as the cars quickly circled. I was grateful that Clarissa and Titus knew a spot like this - one that was still this good of a view.

I took a couple steps away from the rope in a panic as two cars sped by us uncomfortably close.

Clarissa cheered, jumping up and down a couple times as pure joy overtook her expression. I couldn't imagine her ever thinking this was boring if this is how she felt watching.

I, on the other hand, felt surprisingly mesmerized. Once the initial panic subsided, I started watching more intensely. The sheer intensity of the race combined with the real skill it would take to do something like this took me by surprise - I was invested now to say the least.

Searching for Knox's car again, I found him in third place - neck and neck with someone else.

I gripped the rope again, my eyes wide in wonder as the car passing by made the wind whip my hair all around me.

"How many laps do they have to do?" I nearly shouted at Clarissa, barely able to hear myself above the now constant noise.

"I think they're doing 12 tonight. It's not a long race." She shouted back, never looking away from the track.

Titus came to stand on my other side, clearly now more invested than moments before.

I jumped in my skin a second later, a loud bang drawing my attention away from Knox. A car had spun out on the opposite end of the track, smoke coming from both the tires and the engine. I sucked in a sharp breath, grateful it wasn't Knox while simultaneously praying that it wouldn't end up being him either.

I quickly found him again as he whipped by, now in second and trying to pass whoever was in the first position.

I was quickly once again absorbed in wonder as I watched his patient posture, waiting for the right time to make his move. The car in first was doing a good job in preemptively preventing anywhere for Knox to squeeze in effectively.

The crowd was getting impossibly louder as a wave of people moved around. There seemed to be a circle forming in the middle, people frantically moving out the way of whatever was happening.

"A fight." Titus uttered, seeing what I was distracted by.

"A fight?" I frowned. I guess I was foolish to think that an event like this wouldn't have people willing to fight over it.

Titus let out a dry laugh, "Could be anything, everyone who comes to these are bit fucked up in someway."

I chewed on my lip again, how anyone could let themselves get carried away like that over a simple race was beyond me. Returning my focus, gripping the rope tighter as I looked back out at the track.

Just as I found Knox again, he sped up, cutting on the inside of the other car as they both rounded the corner.

"Last lap!" Clarissa shouted to me, clasping her hands together as she bounced on the balls of her feet.

My breathing picked up as Knox was now neck and neck with the other car. It was the last straight before the finish line and both cars were fast approaching.

Just as Knox was about to pull ahead, a loud shot rang out from the crowd. Clarissa screamed in my ear, terror shooting down my spine. Knox's front tire had been burst, making him swerve back and forth uncontrollably. The other car quickly took ahead, crossing first as Knox spun over the finish line seconds behind him.

"Oh my g-" Clarissa breathed out with her hand now covering her mouth.

I gulped, my throat suddenly gone dry. My heart was trying to pound out of my chest and my hands were shaking. My eyes were wide and tears clouded my vision as we watched Knox fly into the middle of the track, eventually spinning to a stop.

I hadn't even realized I was trying to go to him until Clarissa gripped my arm.

"Annie, cars are still on the track, you can't." She shouted.

I nodded my head absentmindedly, unable to move my eyes away from the wrecked state his car was now in.

"He's okay, Annie." Clarissa reassured, still not letting go of my arm.

I couldn't respond, I could barely hear her over the ringing in my ears.

A couple people ran out to his car, opening the door but it was too far away for me to make anything out. I needed to get there. I needed to know he was okay. I don't know what I would do if he wasn't - he has to be.

Once the last car passed, I wrangled my arm away from Clarissa and shot out in the direction of Knox's car.

I sprinted across the track, tears running down my face. My mind spun with all the possible things that could have happened to him - all the worst case scenarios.

The second I saw him standing up, talking to one of the guys who had gone to check on him, I let out a small sob I had been trying to hold back.

Knox whipped around at the sound, furrowing his brows at the sight of me. I ran straight into him, burying my head in his chest as he wrapped his arms around me.

"We - we tried to stop her but she moves surprisingly fast." Clarissa's voice panted behind me a moment later.

Knox didn't say a word back, instead turning with me still latched onto him to continue talking to the guys who he had been speaking with before. His hand gently rubbed up and down my back, soothing me as best he could in this situation.

"No way to tell who took the shot. Came from somewhere in the middle and obviously nobody is fessing up nor do we have any eye witnesses that are willing to admit they actually saw anything." I heard one of the guys saying - picking up the conversation wherever they had left off.

"As expected." Knox grunted back, his arms tensing around me before loosening again.

I sniffled, gripping his shirt tighter. The sound of his voice and feel of his body was all I needed to make sure he was okay. I could feel my body slowly melting into him, the panic easing from my shoulders.

"Here's your cut for second, can't do much else." The other man said, his voice stern and seemingly irritated at the inconvenience.

Knox moved one of his arms from me, taking what I assumed to be money before grunting out a gruff 'goodbye' to the two men.

"Fucking bullshit." Knox ground out, stuffing the envelope into his pocket.

"You good, man?" Titus asked.

"Yeah - nothing new, just fucking stupid. I fucking had that shit." Knox spat. "Where's Sean and Liam?" He asked a beat later.

"Liam got third." Clarissa responded. "Sean was a second behind him, I think they're coming right now."

I peaked out from Knox's chest to see the two of them walking across the track, Liam counting out his own envelope.

"Annie and I need a ride." Knox said once Liam and Sean were within earshot.

"Yeah, I gochu." Liam nodded, his face more serious than I had ever seen before.

Sean looked like he was seething, his face taunt and eyes flaming.

"Fucking ridiculous." Sean spat out.

Knox tensed slightly before nodding sharply.

"Just leave your car for the night. Let's get out of here." Liam said to Knox, nodding in the direction of his car.

25

The car ride was eerily silent. The soft lull of the radio was the only consistent sound besides our collective breathing. Clarissa decided to ride with us as well, taking the front seat as Knox joined me in the back.

I chose to forego the seat belt, needing to be as close to Knox as was respectfully possible. I cuddled into his side, looking up every once in a while to make sure he was still okay. Knox had tilted his head back against the headrest, closing his eyes.

I sighed taking hold of his hand, opting to play with his fingers as I listened to his steady breaths.

We pulled up to my house first.

Leaving Knox for the rest of the night was the very last thing I wanted and although I reasonably knew Serena would not like if he stayed the night, I couldn't in my right mind let him leave.

I looked up at Knox as Liam pulled up to the curb.

It seemed as if my eyes conveyed all the plea they needed to as Knox got out of the car with me, wishing Clarissa and Liam a 'goodnight.'

The lights in the house were all off but the door was unlocked for us - well, me. I glanced around the entry as I stepped in, noticing not even any of the upstairs lights were on.

"She must be asleep." I whispered to Knox as he stepped in behind me, quietly shutting the door behind him.

"Annie, I shouldn't stay." Knox sighed, rubbing a hand down his face.

I knew he was right. I knew he shouldn't. On top of Serena not liking it, he had just gotten into a crash and was probably shaken up. But that was all the more reason why he needed to stay too. Maybe I was being selfish but I know he needs me just as much as I need him.

"Just for a little?" I asked back in a whisper.

Knox thought for a moment before giving me a single nod. With that, I led us up the stairs slowly so as to make as little noise as possible. If not for Serena being such a heavy sleeper, I wasn't sure we'd be able to make it up with these creaky stairs.

Once in my room, I shut and locked the door behind us. Slipping off his shoes and shirt, Knox let out a quiet groan as he laid down on my bed.

I was much slower to take off my shoes, eyeing Knox as I went to lay down next to him. The second my knee hit the bed, his arm shot out to pull me into his chest. He immediately nuzzled his face into my neck, taking a deep breath.

"Are you hurt?" I breathed out, realizing I should have asked this much much sooner.

"Nah." Knox brushed off a little too quickly for my liking.

"Are you sure? It looked pretty bad." I pried further, pulling away from him so I could see his eyes.

"Just gave me a little whiplash, nothing serious. I've been in worse." He confessed, sighing.

I hummed, satisfied enough to let it go for now. I pressed a kiss to his jaw before cuddling back into his chest.

"Annie." Knox called softly.

I hummed in response, unable to peel my eyes back open.

"I need to go, baby." He said.

I frowned, nuzzling further into his arms in protest.

"I promise I'll see you in the morning. You and I both know I can't stay tonight." He sighed, pressing a kiss to the top of my head.

"Fine." I grumbled, letting go of Knox so he could stand back up and go.

I watched, pouting the whole time as he slipped his shirt and shoes back on before walking to my window and pulling it open.

"Sweet dreams, baby." He whispered before climbing through the window and out of sight.

I wasn't aware of when I fell asleep, next thing I knew it was morning and I was waking up to a knock on my bedroom door. Stumbling out of bed, I unlocked and opened the door to a smiling Serena.

I dragged my hand down my face before giving her the best smile I could for having just woken up.

"How was your night?" She asked, walking in and sitting at my bed.

"It was nice. Nothing special, but nice to get out of the house." I said. It wasn't a complete lie, it really was nice being out with Knox but it definitely could have gone better. Serena didn't need to know that, though.

"How was your night?" I asked back, redirecting the focus off of me as quick as possible.

Knox's POV

I was pissed. Last night's crash was the most insane way I've seen someone interfere with a race. I mean a fucking bullet to my tire? As glad as I am that it wasn't worse than that, the whole thing makes no sense.

Having to leave my car there over night also meant that I got a ticket. I just knew my parents were going to have a field day with that.

After leaving Annie last night, I walked to Liam's. It wasn't a long walk, but it was nice to have some alone time to clear my head regardless. Liam wasn't shocked when I walked through his door. He just waved me off to the guest room.

As much as I would have loved to spend the night with Annie, last night was not the right time. I couldn't stay there after everything that had happened, I really just needed to get my mind together. I also knew it'd put me in a bad spot with Serena if she ever found out and the last thing I wanted was to get on her bad side. I just didn't want to risk it.

I called a tow truck first thing this morning, towing it to an auto shop. Liam drove me to the shop while they fixed the tire, leaving it good as new.

"I'm glad you're okay, man. That shit was fucking crazy." Liam said as he drove.

"Yeah, thanks. Weird as fuck for real." I mumbled, still tired as I barely got any real sleep last night.

"Sean's already trying to find out who did it." Liam said.

I nodded my head, grateful to have friends who would look out for me.

"Give him his cut for me, yeah?" I asked, pulling out some of the cash from the envelope before handing it to Liam as he nodded.

Liam dropped me off in the parking lot just as they finished with my car. I paid them and took back my keys before driving straight to Annie's house.

I pulled up to the curb just as I saw Serena leaving the house. She smiled, waving as I stepped out of the car. I thought for a moment that she would stop and talk to me but she just got into her car and pulled out.

I let out a sigh of relief at not being interrogated about last night before walking up and knocking on the front door.

26

----

* Very Mature Scenes*

I ran down the stairs to open the door assuming it was Serena who had knocked thinking she had forgotten something. I stumbled slightly as I opened the door and came face to face with Knox in all his glory.

My mouth formed an 'o' shape as I stared at him blankly.

"Good morning, baby." He smiled softly, planting a light kiss on my forehead before stepping inside.

"Good morning." I all but whispered back. Embarrassment flooded my cheeks as I glanced down at my pink care-bear pajama set that I hadn't yet changed out of.

"Did I wake you?" He smiled, amusement dancing in his eyes as he looked me up and down.

"No." I grumbled weakly, "You always just catch me before I have time to change into something more suitable." I argued pathetically as I began climbing the stairs to my room, Knox on my heels.

Knox audibly chuckled behind me, following me into my room.

"I'm going to change." I glared, turning away from him towards my closet.

"Oh no, Annie baby. Trust me, what you're wearing is perfectly suitable." Knox teased, pulling me into his lap as he sat on my bed.

I groaned, aggressively running my hands down my face. "I'm embarrassed." I confessed, pouting at him.

"I think it's hot but if you're really that embarrassed, you can always take them off." Knox said, winking down at me.

The tinge of my cheeks was now raging, burning my whole face.

"I'm okay." I said softly, averting his eyes.

Knox hummed, smirking. Only a beat of silence passed before his tone turned much more serious.

"I'm sorry you had to be there for that last night." Knox apologized.

I frowned, looking up at him in confusion.

"It's not your fault." I argued.

"I just - I knew I shouldn't have taken you but I did anyways and you had to be there for - for what happened and I am just sorry." He sighed.

"It's not as if anything happened to me, though. I was completely safe and I had a decent time - I'm the one whose sorry that you got hurt. You shouldn't be at all sorry just because I saw it happen." My frown deepened the more I talked.

Knox hummed, "I guess. I just feel bad."

"You don't need to. I was glad that you brought me with you." I assured, planting a soft kiss on his cheek.

Knox nodded, appearing to mull over my words, "Okay." He sighed finally, his shoulders relaxing.

Sliding one of his hands through my hair, Knox gently gripped my neck as he brought me in for a kiss. It started off slow and sweet - savory even. My lips comfortably meshed against his in a blissful peace before we each gradually turned more feverish.

Knox squeezed my neck, tilting my head back with a grip on a good chunk of my hair. He tugged - forcing my mouth open, our tongues clashing as he explored my mouth.

He moved his hold from my neck to my jaw, squishing my cheeks as he pulled away licking his lips. I squirmed in his hold, already needy for more.

"Fucking perfect." He whispered, trailing kissed down my neck. He nipped and sucked as he trailed down, tugging me by the hair to expose more of my neck to his attack. I gasped, gripping his shoulders as I shuddered in his hold.

Knox gripped me tighter, peppering kisses all the way back up before leaving a few pecks on my mouth.

"Look at me, baby." He whispered against my lips.

My eyes fluttered open obediently, meeting his.

"I'm going to fuck you now, baby. Are you going to be my good girl and take it?" He hummed, teasingly brushing his lips against mine.

My eyes widened at the crass nature of his words and yet, at the same time, I could feel the pool already forming between my legs.

I nodded, now desperate to feel him inside me.

"Words, Annie. Are you going to be my good girl and take my cock?" Knox ordered, tsking before asking me again.

"Yes, Knox, please." I all but whined, unable to help myself as I ground against his leg in search of any sense of relief.

Knox immediately flipped me onto my back, kneeling between my legs while he pulled off his shirt. My mouth watered as I stared at him, his eyes darkened as he returned his gaze to me.

Nudging my legs open further, Knox reached for the band of my shorts before sliding them off of me. His fingers teasing my skin as they lightly brushed me the entire length of my legs.

I whined, squirming in need.

"Patience, baby. Don't be a fucking brat." Knox chided, his tone firm yet anything but mean.

Now pushing up my shirt, Knox revealed my taunt breasts before him. They were heavy with need and my nipples were peaked with arousal.

Knox wasted no time taking one in his mouth, swirling his tongue around it before he gently bit down. My back arched off the mattress at the feeling, pushing me more into his mouth. He bit down harder at my reaction, earning a strangled moan from my lips. He licked over the spot again before pulling away and laying soft kisses on the other breast.

"Please." I whined, begging through my panting.

"Please what, baby?" Knox asked, pulling away to look down at me.

My eyes felt glazed over with desperation and my mouth hung open as I struggled to express what exactly I wanted.

Knox gripped my face before spitting into my open mouth, "Swallow." He ordered.

I whimpered, closing my mouth to do as he said.

"Now tell me what you want, Annie." Knox demanded lightly as he brushed his thumb over my bottom lip.

"I want you, Knox - I need you in me. Please." I all but begged, my back arching off the bed once against as he slid his hand down to hold my throat.

Knox groaned lowly, releasing my neck before bringing his hands to his pants. I couldn't look away as I watched his dick spring out from his jeans. My pussy clenched in desire, only further soaking my already drenched panties.

Knox's fingers met my clothed core, making me shudder as he rubbed up and down a couple times. I gasped at the cool air hitting me a second later after he had pulled them away.

He quickly plunged two fingers inside my aching core before rubbing up and down my entire slit - then using my arousal to coat his hard cock.

I whimpered watching Knox stroke himself a couple times before bringing his tip to my center. My eyes rolled back and he massaged his tip against my folds, splaying them more open for him.

"You're mine, Annie. In every fucking way." Knox ground out through clenched teeth as he tried to control himself. "I own every inch of your pretty little mind and body. If anyone ever even fucking looks at you, you don't wanna know what I'll fucking do to them."

I whimpered, grinding against the tip of his cock as his words washed over me.

"You're my perfect girl - my perfect little slut. Isn't that right, baby?" Knox hissed as he slowly entered me, his hand coming back up to grip my throat.

I whined, moaning as my walls stretched to fit him. Tears leaked from the corners of my eyes at the mix of the pain and pleasure.

"So fucking perfect." He groaned, easing himself into me entirely.

I reached my hands above my head, gripping as much of my sheets as I could - grasping for any sense of reality.

Knox moved slowly, letting my body adjust to the intrusion and start relaxing before he picked up the pace.

I couldn't contain the mix of moans and cries that left my lips as he began pumping in and out of me. He peppered kisses all over my face as he began to pick up speed.

"I want you to come all over my cock like my perfect slut." Knox groaned, nipping at my ear.

I cried out as he pulled completely out of me before slamming back inside - hitting my walls. I clenched around his length, feeling my unraveling growing nearer.

"Knox!" I cried out in a gasp, my back arching as his thumb found my clit.

A second later, my entire body was shaking with release - clenching around his cock. A moment and couple pumps later, Knox pulled out of me with a groan - stroking himself as his seed shot all over my stomach and breasts.

27

On Wednesday, I found myself back sitting across from Wendy. I was sweating profusely. My legs kept sticking to the leather of the couch - my skin slowly peeling away from it every time I tried to move.

The clock ticked softly behind her far too slowly for my liking.

I knew this week had been going too well. Moments like these in Wendy's office never failed to bring me back down to a much harsher reality.

"I think it's time we talk about your dad, Annie." She said, her eyebrow cocked mockingly as she poised a pen above her pad of paper.

I shifted again as I bit my tongue.

It would be wrong of me to say that this was my least favorite topic - every topic with Wendy was my least favorite - but it certainly wasn't one that I liked.

"What about him?" I feigned ignorance, my eyes surely glazing over as I tried to suppress every feeling that came along with remembering my dad.

"You tell me, Annie." She returned, "Why don't you tell me a bit more about him." She pried.

I glanced back at the clock. I had only been here for 10 minutes. I didn't have it in me to stall for 50 more. As much as I didn't want to talk, it felt easier than fighting her today.

"I don't remember much." I bit my cheek, looking everywhere in the room except for Wendy.

"Then tell me what you do."

"I don't know what he looked like. I can't remember ever seeing his face." I shrugged.

Wendy didn't move a muscle - it wasn't even worth writing down.

She let the silence hang in the air for several more moments before I became too uncomfortable to bear it any longer.

"The social workers took me away when I was too young to remember." I grit out, growing more frustrated. "All I have from him is a stuffed bunny and half of his genes."

Wendy scoffed at my attempt to brush her line of questioning off.

"He reached out, though. Didn't he?" She continued.

I sucked my teeth, she knew he had. She had heard all of this before - Serena and my social worker had filled her in from my last therapist.

"He sent a letter when I was 8. It wasn't substantial." I grit out.

It was far too personal for me to bring up right now - to bring up to her. The letter meant everything to me. It got me through some of the hardest moments of my life - the hardest moments of living in a system that continued to fail me. Every time I felt alone or lost in the world without anyone to turn to, I would slide that letter out of my diary and remind myself that someone somewhere cared. At least in those moments I could matter to someone.

Wendy slowly jotted down a few lines without batting me an eye.

"He promised to take you home? Said he would do his best to get you out of the system soon?" Wendy pretended to ask.

I looked away - the back of my eyes beginning to sting. He had said those things but I wasn't aware she was filled in quite to that depth. She didn't deserve to know. That was my letter.

"So what?" I muttered.

"So he made some pretty serious promises - promises he wasn't able to keep. How does that make you feel?" Wendy asked with a straight face.

I struggled to swallow the lump in my throat. I could've laughed in disbelief at her question if she hadn't taken me so off guard.

"I think it's fairly obvious." I forced out.

Wendy sighed, "Annie, I'm just trying to say that you've had multiple instances throughout your life where people did not always present themselves as they had promised. In a perfect world your trusting nature would be a gift, but I think it's really coming back to harm you more than you can see."

My entire body was shaking now. I couldn't believe she was actually doing this. She was once again making this about me finally making my own decisions. I had just began to retake control of my life and she was chastising me like a 5 year old who couldn't tell right from left.

"I'm sure you have been doing your best and all, but I know you can only look out for yourself to a certain degree. I truly believe you need to rethink who you put your trust in." Wendy continued beating around the bush but I knew what she truly meant.

"You're talking about me being friends with Knox." I whispered, disbelief saturating my every word. All my tears had now dried up as my shock consumed me.

Wendy pursed her lips but didn't deny me.

"I-I can't believe this right now." I stuttered, my entire body buzzing with both shock and rage.

"I'm not trying to offend you, Annie. I just think you haven't been able to clearly see what I mean-"

"I think I see exactly what you mean." I furrowed my brows. "You're using everything that has happened to me in my own life against me. You think that because a whole bunch of bad things have happened, I can't possibly have any clarity on what I want for myself. I couldn't possibly be able to make my own decisions because I'm just too damaged." I grit out, standing up as I grew more hot with rage.

"Well, guess what Wendy? I may be afraid of men and I may have some issues with abandonment, but that doesn't make me fucking stupid. I know who I am and I know what I want for my life. I'm not some naive toddler who can't take care of themself. I've spent my whole life taking care of myself and I'm not going to stop now. I'm already getting better and its no thanks to you so you can shove your pen and paper up your ass and fuck right off." I spat out before spinning on my heel and slamming the door behind me as I walked out.

Serena looked up at me in confusion as I approached the car. By now tears were freely streaming down my face and I'm sure my face was blotchy from how angry I had gotten.

I slid into the passenger seat - barely containing my sobs- before Serena leaned over and brought me into a big hug.

"Oh, Annie." She soothed, brushing hair as she held me in her arms. "We'll stop for ice cream and you can tell me everything once you're ready." She sighed as she wiped my tears away with the gentle brush of her thumb.

A/N

Hey everyone!

First of all I want to say thank you all so much for the love and support!! Knox's Little Annie made Top 10 in the UK and I'm genuinely so humbled and honored. This book has been such a work in progress but I love it with all of my heart and I'm so thankful to see how much you all love it too. I just finished moving so it was such a pleasant surprise to come back to such overwhelming love. I'm so grateful for each and every one of you and I can't express that enough. I hope you enjoyed this weeks part and I will see you all next Sunday!

28

S erena was appalled when I had told her what Wendy had been doing the past several sessions.

Her exact words being, "That ugly, ugly woman."

I suppose I should have told Serena what was happening sooner but I certainly never expected things to get this bad. Serena was thankfully extremely understanding and overtly concerned.

It was safe to say that I would never be seeing Wendy again.

I had even called Knox that night to fill him in on what had happened once I had calmed down and Serena and I had worked everything out. I may have left out most of the detail pertaining to my father but regardless, he was just as enraged as I had been. I suppose anyone whose character was being attacked in such a way would be that upset.

He had asked if I wanted him to come over, but considering how much I still had to process about the whole situation, I thought it was better for me to that on my own.

However, when Knox picked me up the next morning, he didn't hesitate to pull me into a huge hug that thoroughly managed to ease my mind.

I knew I had been sticking up for the right person and he continued to prove that to me in every moment.

I was grateful when the school day passed uneventfully and quite quickly. It was a holiday weekend so my teachers were all more than satisfied with doing the bare minimum today.

After such intense emotions the day before, I was more than happy to mindlessly float through my classes.

A few hours later, I walked hand-in-hand with Knox as he spoke to Sean and Liam while we slowly made our way out of school for the day.

I was completely distracted, lost in my own mind, when Knox called my name.

"Huh." I muttered, looking up at him confused as I tried to refocus my attention.

"Liam's parents have a house on the lake that we go to sometimes. We're going this weekend so ask Serena, baby." Knox said as he tucked a hair behind my ear for me.

"Oh, okay." I whispered, nodding.

His eyes twinkled as he looked down at me, sending me an easy smile.

My insides warmed, sending blood rushing to my cheeks. I wasn't entirely sure what this weekend would entail but I knew one thing for sure and it was that I definitely wanted to keep seeing that smile.

Serena unsurprisingly agreed to let me go. Although she did seem to be mildly hesitant - probably at the idea of me being alone at a lake house with boys. However, I was grateful she was giving me the opportunity to continue pushing myself. A few months ago, I would have never dreamed that I would be comfortable enough to do anything like this ever again.

Knox picked me up the next morning, throwing my duffle in the back seat as I helped myself into the car.

"Where are Liam and Sean?" I asked when Knox started pulling away from the curb.

"They're driving themselves up. It's just a couple hours away so nothing crazy."

I nodded, letting myself relax into the seat since I knew we were going to be here for a while.

The ride was easy. We had only stopped once to pick up some snacks from the gas station. Traffic was surprisingly light and the view out of the window stayed consistently pleasant the whole time.

As we pulled into a long dirt driveway, I started to get antsy. Even though I was confident in my decision to come, it was starting to actually feel real now. I was going to be staying in a house with multiple boys and who knows who else.

As if he could feel my thoughts forming, Knox gently rubbed my thigh soothingly before shooting me a soft smile. I could already feel my anxiety ebbing away.

We came to a stop in front of a beautiful 2 story home with a large front porch facing a cut out in the trees that revealed the sparkling lake.

The gentle breeze tickled my face as I stepped out of the car. The trees rustled with the promise of autumn's arrival as I stared out at the water that glistened welcomingly. A short dock stood out against the water with a small boat laying flipped over in the dirt directly next to it.

"C'mon Annie." Knox called, holding both our duffles as he started up the steps to the house.

I spared one more glance at the water before falling into step behind him and entering the house.

Warm wood filled the house, the sun bouncing off every surface as it reflected in through the windows.

Liam was in the kitchen with Clarissa. She smiled and sent me a warm wave of which I quickly returned.

I felt my mind ease immensely at the sight of her. Although I hadn't been too worried about this trip, I was more than grateful and immensely relieved to not be the only girl here.

Knox led me through a short hallway to a back guest room. It was small with only enough room for a double bed and a couple nightstands. Nevertheless it was cozy and warm so I certainly wouldn't complain.

Knox dropped both our duffles on the bed just as it dawned on me how we would both be sharing this room. I guess I should have realized this sooner but it was something I hadn't even considered until this very moment.

My face grew flushed and regardless of how far we've come in our relationship, I couldn't help feeling a bit shy.

"You hungry, baby?" Knox asked before turning to look at me. His eyes immediately grew darker - twinkling as they took in the realization on my face.

I blushed deeper, shifting where I stood.

Knox hummed, kissing the top of my head before speaking in a much lower tone than before, "Later, baby. For now let's go eat."

I swallowed thickly, trying my best to brush of the promise of his words.

Knox took my hand, leading me back out to the kitchen where Clarissa was tossing a salad. She turned to look at us as we entered, smiling brightly.

"Liam just put some burgers on the grill so we'll have lunch as soon as they're done." She said, refocusing her attention on the salad she was almost done preparing.

Knox sent me a small wink before heading outside, closing the sliding glass door behind him as he went to talk to Liam.

"Do you need help with anything?" I asked Clarissa.

"No, I got it, thanks." She smiled before continuing, "How're you holding up after the race? I'm so sorry that it went like that." She frowned, sparing me glance as she set the bowl on the dining table.

"I'm doing okay. I was more worried for Knox than anything else but it certainly wasn't the experience I was expecting." I admitted, sighing slightly.

"Ugh, yeah. That was the last thing I think any of us were expecting. I'm still glad you came, though. It was nice to be able to hang out with you. I don't get out much unless it's with Liam so I'm so grateful to have another girl around." She confessed.

I smiled back at her, "I totally understand that. I certainly need another girl to hang out with too."

"I'm sure we're going to become quick friends." She smiled, shooting me a friendly wink.

29

After lunch, we all decided we were going to change into our bathing suits and head straight for the lake.

I finished eating faster than Knox and went to the room to change thinking that I would have a few minutes to spare before he came. However, I had all of 30 seconds - barely being able to find my suit, before the door opened and closed behind me. The click of the lock followed a second later.

"I was going to change." I squeaked, turning to face him as I clutched my swimsuit between my fingers.

"Then change, baby. I'm not stopping you." Knox chuckled, going to his own bag to rifle through in search of his own swim trunks.

I hesitated, glancing between him and the clothes I held in my hands. I shouldn't be embarrassed. He's seen me before but something about changing in front of him felt different. I'd be lying if I said it didn't make me nervous.

I stayed standing still, watching as Knox pulled off his shirt and reached for his shorts before sparing me glance and halting his movements.

"Is my pretty girl feeling shy now?" He tsked, smiling teasingly as his eyes raked my body.

"No." I lied, flushing profusely.

"Oh, no?" Knox raised his brows, stepping closer.

I nervously shifted where I stood but shook my head nonetheless.

"Good girls don't lie, Annie." Knox tsked again.

My breath hitched in my throat as his cool hands met the bare skin of my waist - lifting my shirt up slightly.

"I like when you're my good girl, but maybe I need to fuck the shy out of you first." He suggested, his tone low and serious.

I sucked in a sharp breath at the promise behind his words. My eyes widened in both surprise and desire.

"You'd like that wouldn't you, Annie?" He asked, moving his hands further up my body - caressing my warm skin.

Suddenly forgetting where we were or why I had come into this room in the first place, I nodded my head.

Knox let out a small chuckle, his eyes twinkling before he turned to sit on the bed.

"Strip for me, baby." He all but demanded, his eyes hooded with lust.

I bit my lip, hesitating. He wasn't letting me get away with not changing in front of him like I thought he might. Either way I was positive that Knox would make sure my clothes would come off - the idea somehow making the task easier.

I slowly peeled my top off, letting it fall to the floor along with my bra. It wasn't sexy but I was sure it didn't matter to Knox. His fingers flexed like he wanted to reach out to me but was stopping himself.

My shorts went next, dropping to my feet a few seconds later. My breathing picked up as I hooked my fingers through the straps of my panties. Knox's eyes never wavered, his focus was wholly and completely on me - somehow filling me with just the amount of confidence that I needed.

Before giving it a second thought, I let them drop to the floor like I knew he wanted.

Knox let out a low groan, his eyes taking in my every inch.

Standing up slowly, he took ahold of the back of my neck as he tilted my head back to kiss him. I gripped his shoulders, standing on my toes as he towered over me - dominating my mouth with his tongue. He let me pull away, gasping for breath before he continued his trail of sloppy kisses down my jaw. I whimpered as he bit down on my neck, his fingers flexing over my throat.

Turning me around, Knox gently pushed me onto the bed - making me land on my hands and knees. The sound of Knox unbuckling his belt was soon followed by the sound of his jeans meeting my clothes on the floor.

I started to turn my head in an effort to see but was met with a sharp slap to my bum. I gasped, snapping my head straight again. My breathing grew heavy in anticipation. Not knowing what was coming next was making this all the more exciting.

My pulse raced as I felt the bed dip under the weight of him kneeling behind me. The sound of a wrapper being ripped open causing a shiver to shoot down my spine.

I gripped the sheets as his tip prodded my entrance, slowly teasing me. I mentally prepared myself but couldn't help but cry out as he started to push himself inside me. In an instant, Knox's hand tangled itself in my hair as he shoved my face into the pillows beneath me.

"Shut the fuck up or I'll find something to fill your mouth instead." Knox ground out, sinking himself further into my heat. "You want my friends to hear you moaning while I fill up your pretty pussy with my cock?" He asked.

I did my best to stifle my whine, burying my face further in the soft pillows as my pussy clenched around the intrusion.

"Fuck, baby." Knox cursed out in a groan.

He pulled back before burying himself into me completely - making my eyes water and my moan catch in my throat as I tried my best to hold it back.

He gripped my hips, his fingers digging into my flesh as he pulled me back to meet his every thrust. I gripped the pillows tightly between my fingers, desperate for any outlet of the building pressure.

"My girls not so shy when she's moaning all over my dick now, is she?" Knox said as he slowed down so I could feel his every long stroke. My eyes rolled the back of my head as I panted, my legs beginning to shake.

"You take me so well, baby." He praised before slamming into me completely.

I whimpered, shaking uncontrollably as my climax washed over me.

Knox groaned behind me, continuing to pump through my orgasm until he too tensed and stilled with his own. I laid spent beneath him, letting out a small moan as he pulled out of me completely.

I glanced over as he pulled off the condom and tied it up before throwing it in the trash.

My whole body tingled, slightly numb and already sore. I watched as Knox's back flexed as he once again searched for his swim trunks before pulling them on.

Knox's eyes found me again, a smirk slowly spreading over his face as he took in my exhausted - jelly-like form. A blush warmed my cheeks as I imagined the mess I'm sure surrounded me.

He chuckled, humming to himself as he brushed a kiss against my temple.

"My perfect girl."

A/N

Two parts this week because they were both kind of short! I can't believe we're already almost at 30 chapters and there's still so much to come. I hope you guys enjoyed this part and I will see you again on Sunday!!

XOXO - Katt

30

It was absolutely no surprise that Liam and Clarissa were already in the water by the time Knox and I walked out to the dock. My legs still had a slight shake to them that I hope is way less noticeable than it feels.

"Where's Sean?" I asked Knox as we approached the other two.

Knox quirked a brow but simply shrugged in response.

I frowned but didn't pry any further before setting down my towel on the wood of the dock. I barely managed to stand back up straight again before I was scooped into Knox's arms. I let out a small scream, pinching my nose as he leaped with me into the water.

I sputtered upon resurfacing, taken completely off guard.

Knox laughed, sending me a cheeky smile before swimming off.

The rest of the afternoon was spent swimming in the lake, splashing about.

Clarissa and I were unsurprisingly the first to get out, opting instead to lay on our towels and soak up as much sun as we could. Knox and Liam began juggling a soccer ball on the shore not too long after.

It wasn't until we all had retreated inside and freshened up when Sean finally arrived.

I was cuddled into Knox's side on the couch while playing uno with Liam and Clarissa when Sean barged in with no warning. I jumped slightly in my spot, instinctively moving even closer to Knox. The boys didn't seem to be alarmed at all, though. They didn't even bat an eye when Sean came in with a girl wrapped under his arm.

My eyes widened as I took the two of them in. I glanced at Clarissa who thankfully seemed to be just as equally in shock.

Sean dropped his arm, sauntering in and dropping a single bag at the bottom of the stairs. The girl quirked her lips, not moving an inch from where Sean had left her.

"Liam." She greeted, batting her eyelashes before turning to Knox, "Knox-y."

"Lila." Liam nodded, not looking up as he played his next card.

Clarissa visibly bit her tongue as she glanced at Liam before she too played her next card.

Knox cleared his throat, nodding in her direction but didn't utter a single word.

I frowned. Something about Knox knowing who this girl was did not sit right with me. I shifted, suddenly losing interest in any aspect of continuing this game.

"Beer?" Sean asked, his footsteps heavy as he entered the kitchen.

"Ay." Liam called, sighing as he flung the rest of his cards on the table - effectively ending the game.

"Me too." Clarissa grumbled, following suit before sending another scathing look towards Lila.

Lila scoffed, stalking over to the chair in the corner before plopping down. Just then, she turned her attention to me.

"I don't think we've met before." She said, her eyes twinkling.

I shifted again, pulling myself slightly away from Knox who didn't hesitate to pull me back against him - his arm tight around my waist.

I cleared my throat, choosing to ignore Knox's weird behavior, "I'm Annie." I sent her a wary smile. I was trying my best to be welcoming but I knew I was failing miserably.

"Knox's new flavor I take it?" She laughed, leaning back in her seat as Sean handed her a beer.

My brows furrowed and I tilted my head in confusion. Knox's fingers flexed as they dug harder into my side.

"Flavor?" I asked in confusion, the question slipping off my tongue before I could help it.

Lila grinned, her face crinkling slightly in amusement, "You can't be serious." She laughed.

I was on the verge of asking her what she meant again when Knox stood up, bringing me with him.

Turning to Sean, he spoke in a low threatening tone, "Get her the fuck out of here."

My eyes widened as I glanced between everyone in the room. I held my breath in shock, knowing whatever was about to happen was not going to be good.

"Oh so you both can bring your pussy but I can't?" Sean spat back, standing up too.

"Sean." Liam warned, also standing up as if prepared to stop whatever was going on.

I gasped, taking a half-step back at Sean's words. Knox dropped my hand, stepping completely in front of me. I gulped watching Knox roll his shoulders back as he practically squared up to Sean.

"I said to get her the fuck out of here." Knox warned again, his tone calm and unwavering.

Sean scoffed, shaking his head as he glanced back at Lila who seemed to be reveling in the chaos she brought with her.

Without another word, Lila stood up and carefully set her beer down on the coffee table. Sending everyone a mocking smile, she started walking toward the door. "You coming, Sean-y?" She called.

Sean's jaw ticked as he gave Liam and Knox one more look before he grabbed their bag and followed her out the door.

Nobody moved until we could hear the car pulling out of the driveway and rumbling off in the distance.

Clarissa let out a loud sigh, "Fucking skank." She frowned, standing up. "I'm sorry, Annie. Don't take it personally. She has the personality of a wet rag."

I nodded, still frowning as I glanced over at Knox.

"I think I'd like to go to bed now." I admitted softly, doing my best to avoid eye contact with everyone before turning around and walking away.

My heart beat rapidly as I heard Knox's quick footsteps following me into the bedroom. I thought about closing the door behind me, blocking him from coming in, but my attempt was half-hearted and weak. I barely pushed the door only slightly behind me as I walked in when Knox's hand met the wood to stop it.

I didn't dare turn around - choosing to ignore him, I walked over to my clothes and began looking for my pajamas.

I heard the door close with a soft click. Knox's deliberate footsteps stopping directly behind me a second later.

I shuddered, holding my breath in anticipation. What I was expecting, I wasn't sure.

"I'm not saying I've been a saint, Annie, but I hope by now you see that you're not just a flavor to me." Knox said. His hand reached to my hip, slowly turning me around to face him again.

"Why did she say that?" I asked in a whisper, my voice wavering.

Knox sighed, his thumbs drawing circles into my hips - as much a comfort for him as it was for me.

"Lila likes to hang around the race track. She prides herself on getting what she wants and my lack of interest has been a perpetual shot to her ego. She was doing her best to bring you down with her." Knox explained softly, his eyes never leaving mine.

I gulped, nodding as my shoulders begun to relax.

Lila was beautiful and under any other circumstances, what she said would have intimidated me. However, Knox was right. He's given me no reason to question his interest or feelings for me so it was silly of me to believe her for even a second.

"Why did Sean bring her then?" I asked.

Knox shook his head, clenching his jaw for a moment before responding, "I'd like to know too, baby."